ME *and*

TENNESSEE

SHERIDAN HERNANDEZ

SUMMER'S SON

Me and Tennessee
Published by Summer's Son Books
537 Moriches Road
Head of the Harbor, NY 11780

For more information about our books, please write us,
e-mail us at
info@summersson.com

Publisher's Cataloging-in-Publication available upon request.

LCCN: 2010923531

ISBN-13: 978-0-9838004-0-8
ISBN-10: 0-9838004-0-5

10 9 8 7 6 5 4 3 2 1

Thank you to my family. Without your support, this would not have been possible. Special thanks to my daughter, Nathalie, and her friend Hannah, who made me believe.

Prologue

The cold, hard feel of the gun, though menacing, was also soothing to the boy, as he nervously fingered the smooth metal. His hands shook as he caressed the loaded weapon, his palms sweating so profusely that the deadly steel slipped against his skin. He leaned back against a palm tree and watched as the morning sun poured down on the calm water of the Gulf of Mexico, giving the appearance of sparkling liquid gold. He felt the warmth of the new day upon his face, but the sensation brought him no comfort. He raised the gun's barrel to his open mouth and closed his eyes.

And so it had finally come to this. She was gone, too. His mother was dead, killed. He had not yet reached his fifteenth birthday, but he was now an orphan. He felt completely alone. Once again, tears began to trickle down the bronze skin of his young face. He tasted saltiness and snot as the fluids of his misery streamed into his mouth and blended with the taste of metal. One squeeze of the trigger and he could stop the throbbing ache in his heart and body.

So why, then, did he feel paralyzed, unable to command his hands to do the one thing that could free him from the overwhelming sadness that engulfed him? His throat started to hurt as he tried to stifle the sounds of his sobbing, though on the secluded beach where he stood there was no one to hear his crying. He knew he could not go through with it now, though it would have been the easiest choice. The steel of the weapon scraped his teeth as it exited his mouth. His hand, heavy with the weight of the gun, fell limply to his side. He felt his knees weakening, and he collapsed into the white sand, barely noticing its grainy warmth against his wet face. He drew his legs and hands tightly into his torso, pressing the hardness of the gun into his chest until it hurt.

He didn't know how long he lay there on the beach as waves of angry sorrow washed over him. He had a sense for a while that he was drowning. He had once heard that after the terror and pain of drowning passes, the victim is overcome by a sense of peace as the very life that was his slips away from him. The sense of drowning turned into utter exhaustion, and eventually the boy on the beach felt himself just fading away.

Chapter 1

I was fourteen years old when I first met Tennessee, although he had told me his name was Jed. He had been named after his father and his full name was Tennessee Jed, like the Grateful Dead song, but hardly anybody called him Tennessee except his grandmother.

It was mid July in 2004, and, as in years past, I had recently arrived in Dunedin, Florida, where I was to spend the summer with my grandparents. Debbie and Jack Jones were my mother's parents, and several years previously they had retired to Florida as many Americans do. My grandparents had been old as long as I could remember, and they were as traditional and boring as apple pie and ice cream on the Fourth of July. They went to church and busied themselves with community services, such as volunteering at the garden club and helping at church bake sales. My grandma baked She also loved to quilt and would spend hours quilting in front of the TV, gifting her

1

creations to family members or donating them to charities. My grandpa liked to watch sports, especially baseball. He didn't speak much to me, or even to Grandma, but he could find plenty of words for the TV during a ball game. When he wasn't watching TV, he would read the newspaper. As he grasped the flimsy pages, he would shake his head and mutter, apparently perturbed by whatever it was he was reading.

My grandparents always seemed happy when I came for the summer. They called me Dear and asked how I was doing in school. They would joke that I was growing too pretty, and that they would have to chase the boys away. Even before I arrived for the summer, they would always want to know what I liked for breakfast, so they could be prepared.

As a younger child, I had loved the summers spent with my grandparents. Though my grandpa said little, I knew how much he loved me. He would take me for long walks by the sea where he would buy me giant ice cream sundaes. Inevitably, I would struggle to finish the delectable desserts and he would tease me mercilessly that if I ate any more I would turn into an ice cream cone myself.

Unlike my grandpa, my grandma always seemed to have a story up her sleeve. She would tell me tales of her youth and about my mother's childhood. We spent much of our time together baking in her country-style kitchen. There she would teach me songs that were popular when she and Grandpa were young, or songs from her years as a Sunday school teacher. After an afternoon in the kitchen, we would sit together on the porch and drink sweet iced tea while nibbling on the cupcakes and cookies we had prepared.

But now I was fourteen, and I no longer had a passion for baking and ice cream. As my grandparents and I aged independently, I realized their world was separating from my own. Still, I did not mind that I was to spend the summer with them. I was quite sure that this would prove to be a better option than remaining in London with my parents, who often made me feel like an unwelcome stranger in my own home. My mother and father used to refer to me as a recluse and a misfit, and perhaps it was true, for I had no real friends in England. I was used to being alone. The thought of spending the summer in Dunedin, where I knew not a single young person, did not concern me one bit. In truth, I looked forward to visiting America. My grandparents tended to allow me far more freedom than my own parents did, and I was excited to spend the summer writing, for writing was my true passion.

During those first days after my arrival, I was eager to explore my surroundings. Dunedin is a small, sleepy town on the Gulf Coast of Florida. It lies on the northwestern coast of a tiny peninsula that extends southward to form Tampa Bay. One can imagine that its quaint little downtown once resembled that of hundreds of other small southern towns. But as the town grew, and the tourists flocked in on their weekend excursions, the area became more elegant and refined, with boutiques, art stores, and fine dining.

From downtown, one could look westward and see the tiny marina with its sailboats and fishing boats bobbing on water that glittered in the Florida sunshine. Next to the marina was the fishing pier, extending out into the sea. When standing on the pier, it was possible to look to the south and see the tall, elegant hotels of Clearwater beach. If you looked to the west and north, you could gaze upon the lush, untouched beaches of Honeymoon Island.

I loved Dunedin. It was so different from the sprawling city of London where I lived. There were parks with dense vegetation, wild fruits, and endless trails. There were creeks and lakes and, of course, the beaches and the gulf-view parks, where one could stand and scan the water hoping to see a dolphin or manatee.

My grandparents had purchased a cell phone for me, something my parents had denied me even though every other kid my age seemed to have one. I was free to venture out on my bicycle wherever I wished to go, so long as I stayed within the city limits and checked in from time to time.

I had been in town only a few days, but I was starting to know my way around quite well. It was still quite early in the morning, around eight thirty. I liked the little downtown area at this time of the day. It was quiet, as the stores and restaurants did not open until later. I rode my bike through the sleepy streets, waving at the odd person walking his dog or buying coffee at the boxcar coffee shop. Ahead of me, the Gulf was already shining as sunlight poured down from the east. I headed to the pier for a better view.

As I steadied my bike in the rack, I noticed two boys at the end of the pier. They had three fishing poles mounted as they leaned over the railing. I approached them with some apprehension. I guessed the older one to be about sixteen. He was blond, and his hair was very short, like a soldier's. He wore no shirt, and from his deep tan I suspected he was frequently dressed, or perhaps I should say half dressed, in this manner. He held a can of Mountain Dew in one hand, while the other was stuffed deeply into the pocket of his baggy denim shorts. The shorter one looked younger. His skin was naturally bronze and his dark hair fell to his neck, thick and messy. He wore what looked like a very old, gray T-shirt over khaki shorts that fell below his knees.

I leaned across the railing a few feet from the older boy. The sunlight danced on the gentle ripples of the water. It made me think of fairies darting about the water, sprinkling fairy dust.

"See over there. There's dolphins," said the blond boy. I wasn't sure to whom he was speaking.

"Where?" I asked.

"Look, right there. They'll come up again in a minute, just wait." He pointed, and my gaze followed his direction.

"Oh, I see them," I cried. "That's brilliant."

The other boy chuckled.

"What's so funny?" I asked.

4

"Nothing," he replied.

"I don't believe you," I challenged him.

"Okay, it's just the way you said 'brilliant.' I just never heard anyone use that word the way you did before." He rolled his eyes as he turned from me.

"Well, what's wrong with 'brilliant'?" I asked indignantly. "That's just the way we talk where I'm from."

"If those dolphins come any closer, they'll scare away the fish," interrupted the other boy.

"Did you catch anything yet?" I asked, looking into their empty bucket.

"Nah, this part of Florida's too fished up—it's hard," the blond boy said.

"So what we doing here, then?" complained the younger one.

"What we're doing here, kid, is called fishing. And, like I told you before, it's not about how much you catch. Anyway, nobody forced you to come." He was clearly annoyed by the question. He turned to me and continued, "So, Brilliant, are you from England?"

"No," I said. "I'm from New York. Can't you tell from my accent?"

The boy looked confused. "What, you mean you live in New York?"

"No," I responded, embarrassed that my lame attempt to be funny had obviously failed miserably. "I'm joking," I said. "You know, ha ha."

I waited for the boy to respond, but he said nothing. He just stared at me. The silence between us felt suddenly enormous, and I immediately regretted the ha-ha comment as I realized I had probably sounded as if I was being totally sarcastic. I wanted to kick myself for being such an idiot. "Yes, I'm from England," I said laughing, as I tried to keep the conversation going. I grinned at him,

5

hoping he would do the same. Instead he turned his attention to the fishing rods. "I'm Rachel," I offered. "It's nice to meet you."

"Good to meet you, too, Rachel. I'm Kyle." Much to my relief, he finally did smile in my direction, showing the whitest teeth I had ever seen. That's when I first noticed his eyes were the same green-gray as the sea. For a moment, I was mesmerized and I had to force myself to look away from him. I turned to the other boy. "And your friend, what's his name?" I inquired.

"I'm Jed, Jed Morales. What's up?" The kid nodded, and his dark, uncombed hair fell forward into his face. He pushed it back to reveal deep, dark eyes in the shape of large almonds.

"So are you on vacation?" asked Kyle.

"Sort of," I answered. "I'm spending the summer with my grandparents. They live here."

"Cool," Kyle said.

"Do you live here?" I asked him.

"Yeah," he said, nodding. "Just over there on Bayshore."

"You're so lucky," I said. "I would love to live here. Dunedin is so beautiful."

"You've got to be kidding." Kyle shook his head as he reeled in one of the fishing lines and recast. "I can't wait to get out of here. I already signed up to join the army."

"Really?" I said. I was a little surprised because he looked so young.

"Yeah, for real. I'm leaving for basic training at the end of the summer."

"You're such a loser, man," said Jed. "Only an idiot would sign up for the army."

Kyle prodded his index finger into Jed's chest. "You can be such a little ass sometimes," he snarled. "What the hell do you care? At least I've got a plan to do something with my life, and anyway, what other choices do I have? You think I want to lay carpets for rich people, or take out their garbage, or do any other

6

crappy job like that for the rest of my life? No way, man! Besides, I'm going to fight for *your* freedom, so *you*"—he pointed his finger again, almost touching Jed's face—"should be thanking me."

Jed shook his head. He picked up a skateboard from behind him. "You're going to get your ass shot off in Iraq," he said, before he walked away sulkily.

Kyle watched the younger boy as he left the pier.

"My goodness!" I exclaimed. "What on earth is his problem?"

"It's not his fault," said Kyle, shaking his head and beginning to reel in the fishing lines.

"That's rather big of you to say, considering how he just spoke to you," I replied.

"Look, you don't know anything about him, and seeing as I don't even know you, I probably shouldn't say anything, but that kid's life has sucked." Kyle was gathering up the fishing equipment and was obviously preparing to leave. He rubbed his forehead as if he was worried, which made him look suddenly older. He stopped to look at me. "Look, I feel sorry for Jed. That's why I watch out for him. He's just a kid."

I was surprised and moved by such a display of compassion from an adolescent male. I didn't know very many boys of Kyle's age, but the ones I had encountered in England only seemed to express emotions if the topic involved sports, beer, or teenage girls. I suddenly felt myself becoming nervous and shy. "So how old are you?" I asked. I could feel my heart thumping fast in my chest, and my cheeks suddenly burned hot. I looked out across the water, avoiding eye contact.

"Seventeen," replied Kyle. "How about you?"

I had to swallow hard before I could speak. "Well, I'm...I'm fourteen." I hesitated. "I'll be fifteen before long," I fibbed; I had just turned fourteen a few weeks previously.

"Fourteen, huh?" He chuckled. "Good thing I asked first." He smiled and his sea-green eyes sparkled.

"What do you mean?" I asked. I felt flustered.

"Nothing." Kyle shook his head. "It was nothing. Hey, listen, I gotta go and find Jed, make sure he's okay, you know."

"Oh, okay," I said. I looked down. I felt foolish, like I was sulking. But I couldn't help it. I didn't want him to leave.

"Well, I guess if you don't have anywhere you have to be, you could help me find him," Kyle said, sounding unconvinced.

"Oh, that would be fine," I blurted out. "I mean, I would love to. I mean, I don't have anywhere I have to be, so I can." I could feel my head nodding, and I began to wonder if I had lost all self-control. "Oh wait, what about my bike?" I had forgotten all about the fact that I had ridden my bike to the pier.

"Don't worry," answered Kyle. "We can throw it in the back of my truck."

Kyle gathered together the fishing rods and tackle bag, and began to head down the pier. I followed behind him, consciously taking some deep breaths in an effort to calm myself. "Get a grip, Rachel," I muttered under my breath. *For goodness sake*, I thought, *the way I'm acting, anyone would think I had just met my soul mate.*

After throwing in the fishing equipment, Kyle hoisted my bike into the back of his small, beat-up pickup truck. I joined him in the front cab. It was dirty and smelled like stale smoke. Empty soda cans and beer cans lined the floor. "Just kick those out of your way," he said as he started the truck. The radio began playing rap music so loud that the truck seemed to bounce to the beat. I was about to ask who the artist was when Kyle turned the music down.

"Sorry," he said. "I like my music kinda loud when I'm driving."

"Do you know where Jed might have gone?" I asked.

Kyle shrugged. "Maybe he's walking back to the house," he said. "We can look there first, anyway."

"So how do you know him?" I asked. "He's so much younger than you are."

8

"We live next door to his grandma. She has custody of him now." Kyle turned the truck onto Bayshore. "My house is just a ways up here."

I wanted to ask why Jed lived with his grandma and not his parents, but for some reason I had a sense that Kyle did not want to share this with me. "So what about you, who do you live with?" I inquired, trying to keep the conversation alive.

"Oh, it's just me and my mom."

"What about your dad?" I pried. "Does he live nearby?"

"Yeah," he answered, as he pulled the truck into a small driveway. "But he's a sorry drunk, and I don't see him all too often if I can help it."

I was surprised that Kyle would share something so personal with me, a girl he had just met. I was sure that it was a painful subject for him to talk about, and I wanted him to know that I felt bad for him. But when I looked at his face, he expressed no emotion. And though the tone in his voice had been somehow cold, almost cruel, I felt there was no agenda fueling Kyle's harsh description of his father. I did not get the feeling he was seeking either my sympathy or even a response. I only had the sense that he was being brutally honest about the reality that was his life.

I was not used to this at all, and I didn't know what to say. The way I had been raised, it was simply expected of me to act at all times as if everything about our family, and my life, was perfect. My parents were very conscious of how they were perceived by others, and from a very early age I had been taught that, as their child, I was expected to portray our family as ideal. In a strange way, I sort of envied Kyle's ability to be so open and honest.

I felt a surge of resentment toward my parents as I found myself blaming their pretentiousness for my complete inability to say anything that seemed appropriate at that moment. I so very much wanted to say the right thing to Kyle to show him that I cared.

9

Fortunately the moment of opportunity was fleeting, for I saw with some relief that Kyle was already exiting the truck.

As I climbed out of the truck to join him, I was quite astonished by what I saw before me. "Wow!" I exclaimed. The garage door, by which Kyle had parked his truck, was painted in bright yellow, with enormous orange and pink and red flowers splashed chaotically about it. In the middle was a large purple peace sign. The image, though attractive, seemed oddly out of place and time.

Kyle smiled. "Oh yeah," he said, chuckling. "Jed's grandma is an old hippie. Wait till you see inside the house."

Kyle knocked on the front door and then let himself in. "Rosa," he called. "Have you seen if Jed came back here?"

The house smelled of incense and cloves. I could hear music playing in the background, and I recognized the nasal drone of Bob Dylan's voice. The walls displayed intricate tapestries and framed psychedelic posters with pictures of hairy people I presumed were famous rock stars of decades past. I noted numerous houseplants hanging from the ceiling, and on windowsills and side tables, and many candles of various shapes and colors arranged about the room. The furniture was draped with brightly colored Mexican blankets that clashed with the mismatched cushions that had been carelessly tossed upon them. The room was indeed an ensemble of color and design, and yet it was neat and surprisingly inviting, and I felt quite comfortable as I stood in observation.

"Hello, I'm out back," I heard a woman's voice calling. "Come on around," she continued.

"Come on," said Kyle. He led me through the little house and out the back door. I found myself standing in a small but beautiful patio garden, where an enormous variety of gorgeous flowers of every color blossomed about me. There I saw a lady kneeling down by one of the little flowerbeds. As she stood and turned around to greet us, I was surprised by how young and attractive she was. She appeared to be only in her forties or fifties. She was petite, with long black hair that was dotted with gray. Her skin shone with sweat, and I noticed it was the same bronze color as Jed's. She wore a colorful smock with embroidered pictures on it. I imagined it had been made in a country like Peru or somewhere equally exotic. Her long denim skirt fell almost to the ground, and her hair was held back by a bandana. Large silver hoops hung from her ears. I thought she looked really cool, especially for a grandma.

"Hey Rosa," said Kyle. "This is my friend Rachel." He turned to me then and continued, "Rachel, this is Jed's grandma, Rosa."

"Hi," I said.

"Peace," said Rosa with a smile. We followed her through the back door and into the kitchen, where she offered us lemonade. "No, thanks," we both said, shaking our heads. "Suit yourselves," Rosa said. "Now, what were you yelling at me, Kyle?"

"I was looking for Jed," said Kyle. "He kind of got pissed off while we were fishing, and he took off. I thought maybe he came back here."

"Hmm," grunted Rosa, "my Tennessee pissed off, what a surprise." She had an expression of sarcasm on her face, which matched the tone in her voice. "Well, no, he hasn't come here. What happened to upset him this time?" she asked.

Kyle's expression became serious, and he sighed deeply. "Look, Rosa, don't start in on me about it, but I was telling Rachel about joining the army. You know how Jed is about that," answered Kyle.

"Not just him, Kyle. You know how I feel about that too. I don't think war is justified, especially not the current one in Iraq. And I think you're out of your mind for signing up." Kyle opened his mouth as if he was going to answer, but Rosa interrupted before he could speak. "But I guess you're young and strongheaded and you're going to do what you want." Rosa looked up into Kyle's eyes, and for a few seconds they held eye contact. Then Rosa reached up and gently patted Kyle on the cheek. "You know I love you, kid. I just don't want anything to happen to you." She turned away from

11

him, shaking her head in defeat. "Now, you get out of here and find my grandson, young man," she called back as she walked out to the garden. "And take care of that pretty young lady, too." She looked at me before closing the door. "It was nice meeting you, Rachel."

The expression on Kyle's face revealed his annoyance. "Dammit," he said. "I don't get some people. You'd think she'd be grateful that someone was willing to volunteer to fight for her freedom and protection." He shook his head and laughed the way people do when they see or hear something annoyingly ridiculous. "Instead," he said, laughing again, "she talks to me like I'm some dumb kid who doesn't know his head from his ass. She can really piss me off sometimes."

His obvious irritation moved me. I thought Kyle seemed so mature. He seemed to really know what he wanted and what he believed in. I found him far more courageous and independent than any boys I had previously encountered. But I felt sorry for him, too. He seemed so burdened and serious for someone so young. I wanted to say something encouraging and supportive to him. I wanted him to know how much I admired him.

"I think you're really brave," I said. "I mean, joining the army when there's a war—that takes guts."

I hadn't thought much about the war in Iraq. My parents discussed it occasionally, but they had never spoken with me about such matters. Iraq and Afghanistan, and all the fighting there, had always seemed so far away and foreign to me. But now that I had met Kyle, the war suddenly seemed very real. This boy who stood before me might actually go to war. He could kill someone there, or be killed. "Aren't you afraid you might go to Iraq?" I asked.

"Nah," he answered, shrugging his shoulders. "That's what I signed up for. Whatever happens, happens."

"Really? I think I would be so scared," I said.

12

"Hey listen, I could wreck my truck today and get killed," said Kyle. "At least in the army I'll be doing something worthwhile, and not just wasting my life away for nothing."

"Maybe," I said.

"We'd better go find Jed," said Kyle, changing the subject. "Come on, let's go. I think I know where he might have gone." I followed him out the door and into the truck.

"Um, Kyle? Why did Rosa call Jed 'Tennessee'?"

He began laughing out loud. "Now that's a good question," he said, grinning. "All I can tell you is he's named after his dad, and his dad was named after the Grateful Dead song 'Tennessee Jed'. Ever heard of it?" he asked.

"I've never even heard of the Grateful Dead," I replied.

"Well, if you ask me, you're not missing much. But if you spend much time at Jed's house, trust me, you'll know the Grateful Dead all too well."

"So where do you think he is?" I asked, as we pulled onto Bayshore.

"I bet he's at the guitar shop. There's some fancy guitar there that Rosa's getting him for his birthday. He likes to go there and jam with the owner. He's getting lessons there, too."

"Oh," I said. "When's his birthday?"

"Next month. He's pretty talented with the guitar, considering he's just turning fifteen."

"Oh yeah?"

"It must be in his genes," said Kyle. "Rosa said his grandfather was some rocker dude from some sixties band. Plus, his dad played pretty good, apparently."

"Cool," I said. "Which band?"

"I couldn't tell you," he answered "Rosa never told me. I'm not sure that she's told anyone. It's like she's sworn to secrecy or something. But she claims Jed's grandfather was an awesome musician."

"Well, what about his dad, does he still play?" I asked.

"Jed's dad died before he was born." He paused. "His mom's dead, too."

"Oh my goodness, that's so sad. So that's why he lives with Rosa, I suppose. What happened to them?"

"Maybe you should ask Jed about that," said Kyle. "We're almost to the store anyway."

We pulled up into a little plaza. The letters above the storefront by which we parked read "Creative Strings."

"This is it," said Kyle.

As we walked through the door, I noticed a guy with a ponytail sitting behind the counter strumming an unplugged electric guitar. "Hey Jim," Kyle greeted him. "Is Jed here?"

"Oh, hey Kyle," he replied. "Yeah, he's in the back with Adrian."

Kyle walked to the back of the store, and I followed him. He opened a door marked "studio." Jed sat opposite a gray-haired man of about sixty. Each of them was playing an acoustic guitar, and the older man was singing some kind of blues song. They both looked up at us but continued to play. They sounded really good together. I was impressed.

"I got them low down, low down, way down, deep down blues," sang the man. He ended with a guitar chord, and Jed finished the tune with a short, bluesy riff.

"Awesome!" exclaimed Kyle, clapping.

"That sounded great," I said.

"Thanks, folks," said the man, looking at me. "Who's your friend, Kyle? 'Cause she's too good-looking for you."

"I'm Rachel," I said, smiling.

"Welcome, Rachel. I'm Adrian." He turned to Kyle. "What up, Kyle?" he said, getting up to shake hands.

"Hey man," said Kyle, shaking the man's hand. He turned to Jed. "So here you are, little brother."

"Hey," said Jed. "I see you brought the British along."

14

"I can't get rid of her," Kyle said with a smile. "She keeps following me."

I felt my cheeks flush, suddenly embarrassed, as it occurred to me that I had basically just barged into the lives of these two boys. "I'm sorry," I apologized. "I didn't mean to intrude."

"Hey, I'm kidding," Kyle assured me, a glint of mischievousness in his eyes. I felt my knees weakening. "What the hell, the more the merrier, right?"

I smiled sheepishly, feeling relieved.

"You know, Jed, you shouldn't just take off like that. I was worried about you," scolded Kyle.

"I'm sorry, okay?" said Jed somewhat irritably. "Let's just forget it."

"All right, whatever," replied Kyle. "You hungry?"

"Kind of," answered Jed.

"How about you?" asked Kyle, turning to face me.

"I could eat," I said. The truth was I had no appetite at that moment, but I wanted to go with them.

"Come on, then, we'll go to my place," offered Kyle. "Let's see if my mom's been shopping."

We turned to leave. "See you later, Adrian," said Jed, as he grabbed his skateboard. "Thanks for the time."

"Anytime for you, kid," chuckled Adrian. "Say hello to your pretty grandma for me, and ask her why she hasn't been to see me, okay?"

"Yeah," answered Jed.

"Peace, you guys." Adrian held up two fingers in the peace sign.

"Bye," Kyle and I replied in unison.

We left the shop and piled into the small cab of Kyle's truck. With the three of us in there, I was squished between the two boys. I liked the feeling of them both so close to me, and I hoped the ride would take a while.

In a moment, however, we were back at Kyle's house. It was a striking contrast from Jed's house. The front lawn was almost bare,

15

and what grass remained appeared unhealthy and brown. The small flowerbed by the front door was overgrown with weeds. The house exterior was gray, the paint blistered and peeling. The front door opened into a small living room, with white walls that were smudged with dirt. There was a small sofa and love seat of printed pink and green fabric that was faded and threadbare. In the middle of the room was a light wood coffee table on which sat several small photograph frames. Each contained a picture of a young boy that appeared to be Kyle when he was younger. A small TV sat on a stand by the wall.

I followed Kyle and Jed back to the kitchen. It was a small room with a little dining area to one side. In the dining area was a round aluminum table with four chairs. The blue cabinets with white countertops were littered with piles of paper, but otherwise the kitchen was clean and organized, except for a few dirty dishes in the sink. On the fridge door, I noticed a rather wrinkled flyer with a picture of a red, white, and blue ribbon on it. Underneath the ribbon, the words "Support Our Troops" were written in bold, black letters.

"Is your mum here?" I asked Kyle.

"No, she's working," he replied.

"Oh, what does she do?" I inquired.

"She works in the bakery at Kash and Karry," he said. "She's worked there for years."

"I suppose she must like it okay, then," I said, just trying to make conversation.

"No, she hates it," he snapped. "Her job sucks, but she's got to pay the rent." He looked at me as if I was mental.

Kyle's reaction to my innocent comment surprised and embarrassed me. I felt my cheeks burning with shame as I tried to think of what I might say to correct my mistake. Obviously, my statement had offended him immensely, but I honestly wasn't clear as to what exactly I had said to upset him so much.

16

"I'm sorry," I said, my face still flushed, "I didn't mean to annoy you."

"Forget it," said Kyle, as he turned away from me. "It doesn't matter."

I looked at Jed, who shrugged his shoulders and rolled his eyes. I felt a little relieved knowing I wasn't the only one who seemed to think that Kyle's reaction was a bit weird.

Let's see what we've got to eat here," said Kyle. He went to the fridge and returned to the little table with sliced white bread and a jar of peanut butter. "I guess she hasn't shopped yet, but I think we've got jelly, and there's Mountain Dew or water to drink."

"I'll take a Dew," said Jed.

"Me, too," I added.

After we had eaten, I used my new cell phone to call my grandparents to let them know I'd had lunch and I was at a friend's house. "Do they care that you've been gone half the day?" asked Kyle.

"They don't seem to," I said.

"What are they like, then?" asked Jed.

"They're old." I shrugged. "I don't really know. They bake and watch baseball and go to church. They're nice, I suppose."

"What about your parents, what are they like?" asked Jed.

"They're okay. I mean, they're fine, as parents go. We get along all right and everything. They're just very busy people."

"Do you have brothers or sisters?" asked Kyle.

"No, I think just me was more than they could handle. Like I said, they're very busy."

"Well, what are they so busy with?" asked Jed.

"My mom's an actress," I told them. "She's on this English soap opera. She plays a 'rich bitch American,' my dad says. My dad's the show's producer, and it just takes up most of their time, so we don't get to spend much time together."

"You must be rich, huh?" said Jed, smiling.

"Yeah, I bet you're loaded," said Kyle, as he leaned back in his chair, his hands folded behind his head.

"I never really thought about it," I said. "My parents certainly don't go around saying how rich they are, but I suppose, compared with most people, they're quite well off." I wasn't sure why, but I was beginning to feel embarrassed again, and unfortunately I was quite certain that the redness in my face revealed my discomfort.

"So, Princess, do you eat little cucumber sandwiches and drink tea at the palace with Prince Charles, and crap like that?" Kyle took a swig of his Mountain Dew, sticking his little finger up as if he were some sort of aristocrat.

"No," I said indignantly, "and don't tease me. We live normal lives, just like you."

"I don't think so," said Kyle, smirking. "You have no idea how I live, Princess."

"Don't call me that," I said defensively. I could feel myself becoming flustered.

"Leave her alone," said Jed. "What's it to you if she's rich or not?"

"Fine, *Rachel*," Kyle said sarcastically. "Don't sweat it so much. Anyway, you should be grateful to be rich."

"I am," I said. "I mean, I am grateful for what I have." I looked down at the table. I felt humiliated and hurt. The peanut butter sandwich in my stomach seemed to be expanding, and I felt quite nauseated. Kyle had been so nice to me, and I was really starting to like him. Now I felt like he was making fun of me for something that I had no control over. I just couldn't understand why he was being so hostile.

"I've got to go," I said, getting up. I suddenly felt like I couldn't get away from the two of them fast enough.

"Suit yourself," Kyle said, without looking at me.

"Why do you have to go?" Jed asked. "I hope it's not because of what this asshole said."

"No, it's not," I lied. "I just think I should be getting back." I was already by the door. "Um, I need to get my bike down." I lowered my head and raised my eyes to look at Kyle. I felt like such an idiot.

"Whatever," he said, as he got up and began walking to the door. "You know, there's no reason to get upset. I couldn't care less if you're rich or not." The tone in his voice was suddenly gentler, if a little weary. The feeling of a belt squeezing my chest, which had made breathing difficult, suddenly lessened, allowing me to inhale deeply. Immediately thereafter, though, a sense of dread overwhelmed me as I felt my throat tightening and my eyes moistening. *Nothing*, I thought, *could be worse than if I started to cry in front of him*. I hurried through the door to the truck, swallowing hard to hold back the tears. I wondered what the heck was wrong with me. Kyle followed me, fortunately unaware of my fragile emotional state.

"Hey, I've got nothing, and I guess you've got a lot. It's what life deals you, right?" He shrugged. I struggled with the handle on the pickup's tailgate. "Here, move, let me get it for you," he commanded, reaching in front of me to open the truck. He pulled down the bike and handed it to me. "Are you all right, then?" he asked, looking me straight in the eyes.

"Sure," I said, turning away. I was afraid he might realize how close I had been to losing it.

"Hey Rachel." I turned to see Jed standing by the front door. "Why don't you give us your phone number? Maybe we can hang out again sometime, if you want."

"Okay," I answered, though by now I was nervous and unsure if this was something I should agree to. Jed walked toward me and handed me some paper and a pen. I scribbled down my name and number and handed it back to him. I straddled my bicycle.

"See you," Jed said, smiling. His black eyes seemed to reach into me, taking me by surprise.

"Yeah, I guess maybe we'll see you sometime," Kyle added.

"Yeah, okay," I said, as I rode out of the driveway. "Bye," I yelled, without looking back.

Chapter 2

As I rode my bike along Bayshore, I felt my tears wet on my cheeks. My vision was blurred, and I wiped my eyes. The strangest thing was that I didn't even know why I was crying. Certainly, kids had said worse things to me before than anything Kyle had just said, and yet none of those things had bothered me much at all in the past. So why did I care so much what Kyle thought of me now? I barely knew him. The fact was I barely knew either Jed or Kyle. Yet I felt oddly connected to them, and I did care what they thought of me. I realized how much I hoped that one day soon they might actually care for me. *Perhaps if they get to know me*, I thought, and I really wanted them to know me.

I wiped my nose and eyes with the back of my hand, trying to clear my head and calm myself. I thought I must be some kind of emotional idiot to be acting this way. I was not really an emotional person, and the whole experience had caught me off guard.

Back in England, my parents were always nattering to me that I was too withdrawn and quiet. They wanted me to be more outgoing and to have more friends. It was true that I didn't have many friends. I didn't relate to a lot of the girls I knew. For one thing, I despised shopping. If I could have worn jeans, tennis shoes, and a T-shirt every day, I would have. And the way they acted around boys embarrassed me. Maybe it was because I was scared, but I could never say the bold things they said when boys were present. I'm sure most of the kids thought I was some kind of a freak, but I really didn't care. Being the only child of parents who were both totally preoccupied with their careers, I was used to being on my own. I read like a fiend, and I loved to write, too, especially poetry. That's not to say I wasn't lonely much of the time. I was. I often found myself longing for someone just to talk to. Perhaps that's why I liked to write so much. Writing made me feel as if I had someone to share my feelings with.

I decided to ride my bike to Hammock Park. Hammock Park was one of my favorite places in Dunedin. Through the park ran a small creek, where one might see any number of water creatures, from crabs to snakes to little schools of fish. Surrounding the creek was a lattice of trails, each one boasting a canopy of palms, vines, cypress trees, and wild citrus trees. As I explored the trails, I would peer into the forest, looking for signs of life. There was such a variety of wildlife that could be seen in the park if a girl just kept her eyes open. Each time I visited was an adventure, and many times I had found inspiration for my writing.

I also loved the park because it was a quiet place where I could think. If I really listened, however, it wasn't quiet at all. The air was filled with a symphony of sound. The songs of birds were accompanied by the rhythms of crickets and cicadas, while all the while the gentle *whoosh* of the wind rustled in the canopy. The tapping of woodpeckers was often apparent, and I frequently heard the snap or crack of a twig or branch as the wildlife moved through the forest. But I always felt very peaceful there, and sometimes it felt like I was the only person for miles around.

As I pushed my bike along a trail, I thought about Kyle. This skinny blond teenager who would be a soldier had, in the hours I had known him, impressed me with his maturity, touched me with his compassion, and hurt me with his contempt. Already I wanted to see him again. I experienced such a sense of physical pleasure through my body just thinking about him. I wondered if he had a girlfriend. If he did, she would be older than me certainly. He had made it clear that at only fourteen, I was too young for him. At least, that's how *he* felt.

The afternoon sun was so hot, and the air was thick with humidity. My shirt was soaked with sweat. I drank some water from my water bottle, but it was so warm I felt like I was drinking weak tea. Jed had turned out to be sweet, after all, and his guitar playing was definitely cool. I remembered how he came out after me to get my phone number. When he had looked at me with those dark eyes, it had felt like he was looking right into me. It was like he wanted to get inside me. Though the temperature was in the upper nineties, I shivered.

I could see from the way the sunlight dotted through the canopy that it was late in the afternoon. I wondered what the two boys were doing now. I wondered if they were thinking about me. I suddenly had the dreadful thought that they might be talking about me. What could they be saying? They probably thought I was crazy for the way I ran out of there. I felt my cell phone in my hand. Maybe they'd call. I hoped so. The end of the trail was in sight, and I mounted my bike for the ride home.

As I walked through the door of my grandparents' home, I heard my grandma calling me. "Hello, dear, have you had a nice day?"

23

"Yes, thanks," I answered. I walked into the kitchen where she was washing dishes.

"You must have been having a good time," she said. "You've been gone all day long. Who were the friends you had lunch with?" she pried.

"Nobody you know, Grandma," I answered.

"Well, dear," she said with a tone of caution in her voice, "just be careful who you spend time with. I know you're too clever to knowingly put yourself in any dangerous situations, but nonetheless, I expect you to have good judgment. Not everyone is worthy of your trust, remember."

"I know, Grandma," I said. "Don't worry about me. I'll take care."

"Good," she said, "that's all I ask."

———

When I woke the next morning, the Florida sun was already streaming ferociously through the light curtains that covered my window. I had drifted off to sleep thinking of the two boys I had met that day, and as I recalled their faces I experienced a very warm and pleasant sensation that seemed to spread throughout my body. It was an unfamiliar feeling that excited me, and I savored the moment as I lay there in bed, remembering the day before and hoping the boys would call soon.

After breakfast, I packed myself some sandwiches and drinks and headed out on my bike, my cell phone within quick reach. I had brought my journal, figuring if Kyle and Jed didn't call, then at least I could find a beautiful place to spend time writing. I rode my bike a mile or so toward the Gulf. Behind me the rising sun warmed my back. I went as far west as the land would take me, arriving at a street lined with waterfront mansions. The huge homes stood in parade, each enormous structure flaunting extravagance. Though some were

24

frightfully ostentatious, others were quite lovely, and I envied their owners.

I liked to go out there to the waterfront streets, not so much to look at the mansions, but mostly because of the parks. Between some of the homes were small public parks that accessed the water's edge, providing beautiful views of the Gulf and the tiny islands that polka-dotted the green water.

On this particular morning I noticed several boats parked at one of the small islands. I imagined young, attractive people in revealing bathing suits partying, talking, and dancing on the island's shores. I imagined myself among them. A pretty girl would put her arm around my shoulders and whisper something funny in my ear, making me giggle. A group of handsome boys would observe us, watching us with desire in their eyes. I would smile sweetly at them, knowing I could be with any one of them. I sighed deeply, finding my way back to reality. *That will never be my life*, I thought.

Still, I was content to sit there in the park alone. It was true that the sun's rays were scorching, and the wet air felt heavy in my lungs. But the view was as inspiring as the solitude. I knew I could find poetry in the sprinkled sunlight on the water and in the wisps of whiteness that decorated a sky so blue I thought perhaps it was the color of heaven. Alone, I felt the freedom to experience a certain intimacy with these magnificent surroundings. I began to write down my words intended to reveal the near perfect scene before me, words I hoped would sound as profoundly beautiful as the image they portrayed.

> *Fleeting lights of silver sparkle*
> *On silent ripples barely seen*
> *And gone then*
> *Drifting, drifting*
> *Far, farther yet*
> *Until the blue edge of the earth*
> *Is met.*

I closed my eyes, trying to picture the image I had described. I felt energized and excited. There was a tension in my chest that felt amazing, for the passion of expression allowed me to feel emotions I rarely experienced otherwise. I breathed deeply, nurturing my pleasure.

A large pelican descended suddenly from the sky, diving into the water and ascending with a flapping fish in its beak. The sound of the animal hitting the water startled me, awakening me from my trance. I watched the large bird take refuge on a nearby boat dock, where it swallowed the struggling fish whole, its large, baggy pouch hanging down obscenely. I smiled as I thought how odd it was that a creature could appear so majestic and so bizarre at the same time. I thought back to the day before, and my first impression of Kyle. I had so admired him for his maturity and compassion, and yet shortly thereafter I had been so disappointed and hurt by his animosity toward me. I wondered what he was doing. I touched the phone in my pocket, willing it to ring, holding my breath.

The sound of the phone's ringtone startled me. Though I had wished for that sound, I had not expected to hear it. As I pulled my phone toward my ear, I noticed my hand was shaking.

"Hello," I said.

"Hey," said a voice, "it's Jed. What are you doing?"

My heart was pounding, and at first I had trouble finding my voice. It felt like the air was stuck at my vocal cords. I cleared my throat. "Oh, nothing," I said. "I'm just hanging out at one of the waterfront parks. What about you?"

"Me, too. I'm just hanging out," he replied. "Are you by yourself?"

"Yeah," I answered.

"You want to hang together, then?" he offered.

"Um," I hesitated, "is Kyle there?"

"No, he's working now, and I think he's going to Clearwater Beach with his friends later. Why? You're not still pissed, are you?" he asked.

"Oh, no," I said. In truth, I was disappointed. I really wanted to see Kyle more than Jed. "No," I reiterated. "I was just asking. Where are you?"

"I'm at my house," Jed answered "You want to come over?"

"Yeah, okay," I said. "I've got my bike. I'll be there soon, okay?"

"Do you know where my house is?" he asked.

"Yeah, remember I was there yesterday with Kyle and your grandma."

"Right," said Jed. "Well, hurry up. I'm bored here by myself."

As I steered my bike down Bayshore, I began to imagine what it would be like to hang out with Jed alone. This was the first time I had ever spent time alone with a boy, and I felt very nervous. I started to think about what I was wearing. I worried that my cutoff jeans and old tank top weren't exactly flattering. My hair was pulled into a braid because of the heat, and my grandpa had forced me to wear one of his old baseball caps for "sun protection." I was sure I looked anything but attractive. I considered going home to change, but I knew how long that could take, and I really didn't know what to wear anyway. "Oh well," I said to myself. I thought about how stupid I was being. After all, it wasn't as if I was going on a date. I was just going to hang out with Jed, and he probably only called me because he was bored and didn't have anything else to do.

I pulled my bike into his driveway and left it leaning against the freaky garage door. I rubbed the back of my arm across my forehead to remove the sweat, but realized it was useless. My whole body was sweaty and sticky. I removed the baseball cap and let my hair down, running my fingers through to release it. My heart was beating so hard and fast. I didn't know if it was from riding my bike in the

27

heat or because I was so nervous. As I approached the front door, I noticed I was biting my lip. I stood there in front of the door for several seconds trying to calm myself, unsure if I even had the courage to ring the bell. I didn't have to. Suddenly the door opened. Jed looked surprised to see me standing before him. His dark hair was wet, and water dripped onto his face and shirt.

"Hey," I said, "how come you're all wet?"

"Oh," Jed said, looking a little confused. "You got here faster than I expected. I just got out of the shower. I was coming out to wait for you. Um, come on, let's go inside. It's freaking hot out here." He turned and headed into the house before I could answer, and I followed him inside. I noticed his feet left wet footprints as he walked. He wore long, baggy shorts that hung low on his hips and covered his knees. His white tank top contrasted sharply with his coffee-colored skin. He smelled like soap and shampoo. "You must be really hot," said Jed. "Do you want something to drink?"

"Water's fine," I answered. I followed Jed to the kitchen and watched him throw a couple of ice cubes in a glass and fill it with water from a jug in the fridge.

"Come on, I'll show you my room," he said, handing me the glass of iced water.

I followed him through the kitchen and into his room. The room was quite small, with a window that looked out to the back garden. The walls were hung with posters of long-haired rockers, few of whom I recognized. The single bed had been made in a hurry, and CDs lay scattered on the tile floor by a CD player.

Jed looked me briefly in the eye and turned away. "You can sit on my bed if you want," he said without looking back at me.

"What kind of music do you like?"

I sat on the bed and pulled my legs to my chest. Between the air conditioning and the water, my body had cooled significantly. I could tell my heart rate had come down, and I almost felt a chill. I realized I was trembling slightly.

Jed was kneeling on the floor, looking through the CDs. "Do you like any classic rock? I've got a ton of it, you know, from my grandma. A lot of it's pretty fly. I could play you some amazing guitar stuff, like from Jimi Hendrix." He looked back at me, smiling enthusiastically.

"That sounds great," I said. I felt a little embarrassed that I was pretending to know who he was talking about. I'd never even heard of Jimi Hendrix before that day. I didn't really know much about music, except for the pop music that was played on the radio back in England, and some of the classical music my dad listened to at home. Jed put on the CD and turned up the volume. For the first time in my life, I heard the sounds of Jimi Hendrix's fingers manipulating the strings of a guitar, coaxing the notes to sing, then weep, and ultimately scream their story.

"This is amazing!" I said.

"I know," Jed replied as he sat on the bed. He leaned against the wall and began to play air guitar in time with the music.

"So is all this music your grandma's?" I asked.

"No, a lot is mine, too. But she's really into music and she's collected a lot in her life," he explained.

I thought about my grandparents and how completely different they were to Jed's grandma. I wanted so much to ask him about her, and about himself and how he had come to live with her. But I was scared. I remembered Kyle telling me how hard things had been for Jed and that both his parents were dead. I was afraid to ask him anything that might remind him of the sad things in his life. Even though I was cold, I felt my hands sweating.

"What are you thinking?" Jed asked. He smiled slightly and looked me directly in my eyes, holding his gaze. I had the same feeling I had had the day before, as if he was reaching inside me. I looked away, hating how easily I blushed. When he looked at me like that, I felt as if he could see what I was thinking. "Tell me," he said. "Tell me what you were thinking."

"I was thinking about you," I said.

29

"What?" he asked curiously.

"I was wondering why you live with your grandma," I said. I felt somehow guilty for saying this, as if I was manipulating him into telling me about his parents and what had happened to them, because I lacked the courage to ask him specifically.

"Well," he said, "do you want the long version or the short version?"

"What's the short version?" I replied.

"Simple," he said. "I don't have any other family I can live with."

"So what's the long version?" I pried, without making eye contact. I waited for Jed to begin talking, but all I heard was Jimi Hendrix. I looked up at him and saw him watching me. I felt him reading me, studying me.

"How much do you know already?" he asked knowingly. I felt a sudden of pang of shame, as if I'd been caught snooping through someone's personal things. I looked away. "Well, I know your parents passed away," I confessed. "Kyle told me. But that's all he told me. I really don't know anything else."

"Look, I don't care what you do and don't know," he said. "And I don't mind what you ask me. I don't even mind telling you. Just be straight with me, if you want me to be straight with you." He said this with such authority and seriousness that I felt like an adult was chastising me.

"I'm sorry," I said. "I didn't mean to... you know, not be straight with you." But of course, that wasn't entirely true, and we both knew it.

"Whatever," he said. He sighed deeply. "Why don't I just start at the beginning?" He looked at me and smiled. He smiled in a way that someone does when they accept defeat gracefully. It was the kind of smile that says, *yes, it sucks, but what can I do about it?* Still, I thought it strange that he could smile at all when he was about to talk about his dead parents.

30

"My dad died before I was born," he began. "He was on his way to Massachusetts from Florida to marry my mom. He got in a car accident and was killed pretty much right away. My other grandmother, my mom's mom, said he was smoking weed. I don't know if that's why he crashed, but it doesn't matter now anyway."

"Your mom was pregnant before she was married, then," I stated. Jed looked at me as if I had celery stalks sticking out of my ears.

"Well, duh," he said sarcastically. I was embarrassed that I had stated the obvious.

"All right," I said. "I guess that was a stupid thing to say. So how old was he?"

"He was eighteen and my mom was seventeen," he answered.

"God, he was so young. And your poor mum." I imagined the injured teenager being pulled from his wrecked car on the highway, and his pregnant girlfriend hearing the bad news. "That's so sad."

"Yeah well, that's what happened. Anyway…" he said. He turned away from me, and I had the feeling he was trying to clear the image of the accident from his mind.

"So how did they meet each other?" I asked.

"My dad was living here with my Grandma Rosa," he explained. "He worked as a lifeguard down at Clearwater Beach. My mom came down here on vacation with her parents. I guess my dad and her hooked up. When she went back to Massachusetts, she found out she was pregnant." He shrugged his shoulders. "A few months later, here I was."

"Wow," I said, more to myself than to Jed. It almost scared me imagining how quickly people's lives can change so drastically. "What did your grandparents say when they found out your mum was pregnant?"

"Well, obviously I don't really know, seeing as I wasn't even born, but I can only tell you some of what I've heard over the years. My mom told me that at first my grandma was insanely pissed. She

31

actually slapped her across the face and called her all kinds of names and crap. But after a while, she actually seemed happy about it." He paused. "Until my dad got killed, that is."

"Well, yeah, I can't imagine anything worse."

For a while, we both said nothing, and I was sure Jed was imagining how things might have been different if his dad had not died. Eventually I spoke again.

"What about your mum's father? What was his reaction?" When I asked this question, Jed's facial expression changed and he appeared more melancholy. He looked away. "I'm sorry, Jed. You don't have to tell me if you don't want to." I could feel myself becoming emotional in response to him, and I also felt a little guilty that it was my fault he was thinking about all these painful memories.

"It's okay," he said, turning back to me. His eyes looked sad though he showed no tears. "It's just that my grandpa…" His voice cracked. "He's kind of got mental problems. He went to Vietnam when he was really young. When he came back, he had post traumatic stress disorder or something. Anyway, I guess he just kept getting sadder and more wacko. The psychiatrists said that maybe he was already kind of crazy, and the war just made him, you know, even crazier. But I think it was all the bad crap he saw in Vietnam that made him that way." As Jed spoke, he picked at some loose threads that hung from his shirt. I felt as if he was trying to avoid looking at me. "Anyway, the point is," he said as he raised his eyes to mine, "he couldn't deal with my mom getting pregnant."

I gasped. "What, did he kill himself?" I asked, horrified.

"No!" He looked at me with an expression of contempt. "No, of course not." I wanted to apologize, but before I had a chance he shook his head and continued. "No, he had to go to a mental hospital." He paused, as if he was thinking about what he was saying. His eyes became glazed, and I felt like he wasn't really seeing me anymore. "The truth is he can really be a great guy sometimes. After I was born, he

32

really loved me. When I was growing up, he was like a father to me. He did have his problems quite often though, and sometimes it got really bad, and I mean *really* bad. But then some days, we had great times together. I miss him a lot."

I looked into Jed's eyes and for a split second he looked much younger and more vulnerable than he had before. At that moment, I felt as if he were a million miles away from me. I noticed I was holding my breath to avoid making any sound, somehow afraid I would disrupt his thoughts. And then suddenly it was over and he was back in the room with me. He smiled as if he was just noticing me. "Anyway," he said, "what were you asking?"

"Nothing," I said. "But you were saying how your grandpa had to go in the hospital after your mum got pregnant. I suppose your mum must have felt really guilty then, like it was her fault?"

"I don't know. I guess," he said. "I mean I'm sure she was worried about my grandpa, and she probably did feel guilty about what happened to him. But sometimes things happen for a reason."

"What do you mean?" I asked.

"Well, she always told me that even though I was an accident, she never regretted having me. And she said she really did love my dad and that he was happy they were going to get married."

I nodded, thinking how sad it was that the marriage had never come to be. "Well, where's your grandpa now?" I asked apprehensively. Before Jed could answer, there was a knock at the front door. The visitor didn't wait for us to answer; the door immediately opened, and I heard Kyle's voice calling for Jed.

"Are you sure you don't want to come, Jed?" Kyle yelled. I could hear him walking through the house toward Jed's room. I felt the tension in my chest as I anticipated seeing Kyle again. Jed's bedroom door opened. "I heard your music playing," said Kyle as he walked into the room. He stopped abruptly when he saw me. "Oh," he said. He looked surprised. "I guess that's why you didn't want to come to the beach with us then, huh?" he said, smiling. "I

33

agree she's better looking than I am," Kyle winked at me, and I smiled.

"Whatever," said Jed, looking both embarrassed and slightly annoyed.

Kyle ignored Jed's tone. I got the feeling that he was used to putting up with the younger boy's hostility. "Well, you're both still welcome to come, if Rachel's allowed," he offered. "The guys are outside."

"We're fine here," answered Jed.

"What about you, Rachel?" asked Kyle, turning to me. "You want to come to Clearwater Beach with us?"

I could feel both boys watching me, and it made me feel incredibly uncomfortable to be put on the spot like that. On the one hand, I really did want to go with Kyle and his friends. But I felt horribly guilty. Jed had made it painfully clear he did not want to go, and after all, he was the one who had invited me out to start with. "Don't worry about what he wants," said Kyle. "I'm asking you."

"Yeah, go if you want," said Jed sulkily.

"Why don't we go?" I practically pleaded with Jed. "I haven't even been to the beach yet this year."

"Fine," Jed answered sullenly. He got up to turn off the music. "Are you even allowed to go?"

For a moment I hesitated. My grandparents had told me not to go beyond the city limits, and that did not include Clearwater Beach. "Yeah, why not?" I said. If I felt guilty at all about lying, it was for less than a second.

"Are you wearing a bathing suit under your clothes by any chance?" asked Kyle.

"I don't really need one...or maybe I'll just buy one," I answered. I thought it best not to mention that my parents had given me a credit card to use when I needed something.

"Hurry up, then," said Kyle. "We've got to start heading to the beach now if we're going to have time to enjoy the day." Jed and I

34

grabbed some towels from the linen closet and followed Kyle out to his truck. I sensed Jed sulking behind me. I ignored his moodiness. I was really too excited and nervous to care. Just the thought of hanging out at Clearwater Beach with Kyle and his older friends thrilled me.

Chapter 3

As we approached the truck, I noticed two kids sitting in the cab. In the middle sat a girl. She looked about the same age as Kyle. Her blond hair was pulled up behind her head with a clip, and from what I could see she was already in her bikini. The boy who sat next to her had a lit cigarette in his hand, which he held out the window. In the bed of the truck sat a huge man. He looked older than the others, and I thought he must have been well over six feet tall and at least 250 pounds. I began to feel very intimidated. What if they all thought I was just a little kid? I managed to smile, although at that moment I was far too shy to say anything to anybody.

"Hey, you guys," said Kyle to his friends. "This is Rachel, the kid we met yesterday that I was telling you about." I wondered what Kyle had been telling them about me. I recalled how he had teased me the day before.

"Hi, Rachel," said the girl. "I'm Brook." She looked past me toward Jed. "Hey, Jed, how're you doing?"

"Fine," he answered abruptly.

"What's up," said the boy as he blew smoke from the side of his mouth. I looked at the big guy in the back. He smiled at me and winked.

"Hello," I said, half raising my hand to wave. In front of these older kids, I was very self-conscious of my youth, and I felt almost foolish as I stood there trying to act naturally.

Kyle opened the passenger door. "Could you two sit in the back with Hunter so the kids can sit up in the cab with me?"

I slid into the middle of the cab and Jed climbed in next to me. As Kyle took his seat and started the truck, I felt the warmth of his body against me. The heat seemed to penetrate my skin and move through me. I felt exhilarated. Rarely in my short life had I felt so excited, and the anticipation of what lay ahead invigorated me. As Kyle manipulated his little truck southward along Edgewater Drive, I admired the green-gray color of the satin water shimmering to my right. I leaned back against the seat and shifted a little closer to Kyle, absorbed in my own pleasure. Jed leaned forward and turned on the radio. Rap music blasted through the speakers, shocking like a bolt of electricity.

"Why do you like that crap?" Jed asked belligerently.

"Because I think it's good music, man, and it's got a good beat." Kyle looked at Jed, obviously agitated by the question.

"It sucks," said Jed cantankerously. "Don't you know you can't spell the word crap without rap?"

"*That's funny*," said Kyle sarcastically. "What's your problem anyway? You're being such a little butthead today." Kyle scowled, frustration apparent on his face.

"Whatever." Jed rolled his eyes and adjusted the radio. He tuned it to a rock station that was playing an old song I actually recognized.

38

"I don't get you, man. The Stones are older than your grandmother." Kyle shook his head.

"So?" said Jed, drumming on the dashboard in time to the music.

The arguing made me uncomfortable. My mood was being spoiled, and I felt myself becoming annoyed with both boys. "It's really not that important," I said. "It's only music."

Jed turned to me. He looked concerned. "Rachel," he said with a chastising tone, "don't say that."

"Don't say what?" I asked, puzzled by his response.

"Music is like…" He paused as if lost for words. "It's like expression from the soul."

"Well, I suppose I just don't get it then," I said a little defensively.

"I should have warned you about Jed and his music," interrupted Kyle. "He takes it very seriously. Trust me. You don't want to go there. I've made that mistake myself."

"What?" said Jed, shaking his head. "I'm not that bad."

Kyle laughed. "Oh yes you are, little brother. You sure are."

We rode on without further conversation, though the radio remained tuned to classic rock and Jed continued to tap out the rhythms on the truck door.

As we crossed the new Causeway Bridge, I was full of anticipation. The salty air blew in through the open windows, and I smelled the seawater. Below us, I saw numerous boats and jet skis darting in all directions. Ahead of us, stretching both north and south, were the luxury hotels and condominium buildings of Clearwater Beach. When we came to the end of the causeway, we turned right and headed north. Kyle pulled the truck into a beachfront parking lot. "Okay, we're here," he said. "Let's get this show on the road." He and Brook gathered blankets and beach bags from the back of the truck and headed to the beach. The other two boys carried a large cooler between them. It looked heavy. Jed and I followed behind them. He told me that the thinner boy, who was smoking again, was called Tyler. The bigger one was named Hunter.

"How old is he?" I asked. I was curious because to me he looked as if he was in his mid twenties. He had at least a day's worth of stubble on his face and a protruding belly that only exaggerated his already massive frame.

"He's nineteen," answered Jed. "I know he looks older. He doesn't even usually get carded in bars or liquor stores. He has a fake ID anyway."

"What do you mean?" I asked. "How old do you have to be to drink here?"

"Twenty-one."

"Oh really? The drinking age is only eighteen in England," I explained.

"Well, in that case," said Jed, smiling mischievously, "I'm moving to England in just about three years."

As we walked onto the beach, I stopped to take off my shoes. The white sand was so hot it hurt my feet, but it felt good. The sand of Clearwater Beach is so fine that it molds to your feet and seeps between your toes. With each step, I pressed my feet into the sand, enjoying the sensation. I observed the green-gray seawater spread out like a giant blanket before us. The gulf water was so calm that the only waves resulted from bathers playing in the water. We lay down our blankets and Brook began applying sunscreen to her body. Tyler offered to help her and she accepted with a flirty smile. As I didn't have a bathing suit, I tied the bottom of my tank into a knot beneath my bra. Kyle applied sunscreen to his own body and then asked me if I would like some.

"Thanks," I said, smiling as I turned my back to him and lifted my hair. I felt the cool cream touch my upper back and then Kyle's hands were massaging my neck and shoulders. The silky lotion enabled his soft hands to slide across my skin, giving me shivers. I heard him squirting more lotion, and then his hands rubbing together. I waited, holding my breath. I felt his touch on each side of my waist. His hands felt firm, their movements deliberate. He drew the cream in toward my spine, and downward, into the small of my back, and his fingers slipped just inside the top of my cutoffs.

"How's that?" he asked as he moved in front of me and handed me the bottle. "You should be able to do the rest yourself, I think."

"Oh yes, thanks," I answered in a tiny voice. I looked up into his eyes, and he smiled.

"Are you okay?" he asked, still smiling.

"Yeah, I'm fine," I lied. But I was sure he could see my heart pounding through my chest and the shaking of my hands. "I'm just hot."

"Okay then," he said, winking and turning away. "I'm going swimming—who's coming?" He began running toward the water, and Brook and Tyler followed him, laughing and screaming as they raced each other.

"You're not going in?" asked Hunter. He was lying on the blanket, and he used his hand to shade his eyes from the sun as he looked at me.

"I don't know. Maybe later, but I don't have a proper suit."

"So what?" He laid his head back on his hands and closed his eyes. "In this heat, you'll dry out quick. Besides, I bet you'll look hot with your shirt wet." I felt my face flush. Jed muttered under his breath.

"You say something, Jed?" asked Hunter, opening one eye to look at him.

"I said you're a pig."

"What, you don't think she'll look good in a wet shirt?"

"Why do you have to be such an ass, man? Leave her alone." It was obvious that Jed did not think very highly of Hunter.

"What?" Hunter laughed, and the gurgling sound that he made was somehow ugly and offensive. "I gave her a compliment."

41

"It's all right, Jed," I interrupted. "I don't care." But in truth, I felt humiliated. Not only by Hunter, but by the two of them, and the way they had talked about me while I just sat there. They acted as if I couldn't hear what they were saying.

"See?" said Hunter. "She's into it, aren't you, Rachel?"

I pretended not to hear him. "I'm really thirsty," I said.

"There's soda in the cooler," said Hunter. "Jed, give her a drink of something, and get me a beer while you're at it." Jed listed the drinks in the cooler, and I asked for a Diet Pepsi. He tossed a can of Budweiser to Hunter. I leaned back on my elbows and looked out at the water, observing people splashing and squealing in the gentle waves, while the boats in the distance moved slowly across the horizon.

Jed was lying on his belly next to me. Suddenly, he propped himself up on his elbows. I heard him clear his throat. "So," he began, "what do you do for fun in England?"

"What do you mean?"

"You know. Who do you hang out with? What are your friends like? What do you guys do over there?"

"I don't know...I don't really hang out that much. I have a lot of schoolwork." I knew that my feeble excuse for my pitiful social life was pathetic.

"Well...do you have a boyfriend?"

"Not really right now," I answered. The statement was dishonest. It implied that I had had something that at least resembled a relationship with a boy. I hadn't. "What about you?"

"Nah," he replied, shaking his head. "I've never had a girlfriend before."

I rolled onto my belly and propped myself on my elbows closer to Jed. I wasn't sure if Hunter was asleep, and I didn't want him listening to our conversation. "Jed," I said.

"Yeah?"

42

"How did your mum pass away?" Jed remained silent for a while, and I thought perhaps he wasn't going to answer me. "You don't have to tell me," I said.

"No, I don't mind talking to you about it. I just don't know how to answer that question sometimes" Jed turned to me and looked into my eyes. I felt as if he was searching me. I looked away, not really sure what to say.

He sighed and looked down toward the sand. "The military has it on record that she died of pneumonia. As far as I'm concerned, she was killed when she was in Iraq."

"She was in the army?" I was shocked. But I now understood Jed's objection to Kyle's signing up.

"She was in the National Guard," said Jed. "I don't think she really thought she'd ever get deployed to a war zone. She would never have signed up otherwise. Anyway, she was sent to Iraq almost two years ago now. I guess one day she was on some kind of a mission or something. Her vehicle was hit by a roadside bomb and blew up. Her head got smashed in. She survived, though, and they flew her to Germany for surgery. But after that, she was, you know, like a vegetable. A couple of months later, she was sent to a rehab center in Washington. The doctors said she"—he hesitated—"what's the word they used? *Aspirated.* That means sucked puke into her lungs. That's how she got pneumonia. Anyway, I don't think she ever came back from Iraq...not really."

My throat tightened as I struggled to hold back the tears I felt pricking at my eyes. "I am so sorry," I said, turning my body to face him and hastily wiping my cheeks. His face expressed no emotion. He looked right through me. I wondered if he was picturing his young mother wounded in Iraq. He sighed.

"So my grandfather lost his mind in one pointless war, and my mother lost hers in another." He shook his head in disgust. "It's so freaking stupid."

43

"You should be proud of both of them," Hunter interrupted without raising his head or opening his eyes. "They fought for their country and for freedom. That's honorable."

Jed sat up quickly. He appeared angry. "Tell me what the hell those wars did for me. Show me how they've affected my freedom except for taking away my mother."

"It's all right, Jed," I said, sitting up. I was concerned by how emotional he had become.

"Calm down, little dude," said Hunter. "Don't freak out."

"Then just shut the hell up," growled Jed.

Now Hunter sat up abruptly. "Just remember who you're talking to. I could squash you like an ant."

"He's just upset," I said. I felt a little panicked. The situation seemed to be escalating out of control. "Can't you show some compassion? You don't have to be so mean to him." I wasn't usually so assertive, but I couldn't help myself. I couldn't just watch this giant bully upset Jed. The boy had already suffered so much. Perhaps it was what I had said, perhaps not, but Hunter got up then. "Losers," he said as he walked away.

"Asshole," responded Jed.

I turned to face him. As I reached out to touch Jed's arm, I heard someone yelling my name. I turned toward his voice and saw Kyle, Brook, and Tyler bounding toward us. "Rachel," Kyle yelled again, "come in the water. It feels great." I was about to decline when he ran straight to me and scooped me up, throwing me over his shoulder and running back toward the sea. I squealed with delight, instantly forgetting the conversation with Jed.

As Kyle ran with me, I could feel my stomach pressed hard into his shoulder and his arms and hands wrapped tightly around my thighs. With each step, I felt the shock of the impact deeply in my belly, but I was experiencing such pleasure in the physical closeness that I disregarded any discomfort. He ran straight into the water, lifting his knees high with each step. As he moved deeper into the sea, I felt the warm water splashing me. I tasted the saltiness on my lips. Suddenly he fell forward. As he fell, I felt myself falling backward with him, sinking into the water, the weight of his body completely submerging me. I closed my eyes and held my breath. Beneath me I tried to feel for the seafloor with my feet. And then I felt Kyle's arms reaching around my waist and pulling me to the surface. He pulled me close to him. "I'm so sorry," he said, laughing. "I swear I wasn't trying to drown you. Are you okay?" He gently pushed me away from him and looked at me, smiling as he checked my condition.

I pushed my wet hair away from my face and rubbed the seawater from my eyes. "I'm fine," I said, laughing, enjoying the feel of his hands on my skin. "Actually that was fun, and you're right, the water feels great." It was true. In midsummer in Florida, the heat and humidity can be oppressive. Each day the temperature reaches the mid nineties, and at night the air only cools to the seventies, so the gulf waters heat up. After roasting under the hot sun, bathing in the sea was pleasantly cooling.

Kyle let go of my waist and sank down into the water until only his head was not submerged. "I told you it would feel good," he said, smiling. "So you and Jed seem to be getting kind of close, huh?" He cocked his head to one side and peered at me through squinted eyes.

"Sure, I guess." I wasn't sure what to say. I did feel as if I was becoming close with Jed. I truly felt that I was starting to care about him, and I felt a bit guilty that I had just left him sitting back on the beach after he'd confided in me. But I didn't want Kyle thinking that something more was happening between Jed and me. After all, it was Kyle that I liked. "Jed's a sweet kid, even though he's a bit moody," I said, hoping I sounded mature. "He was telling me about his parents and everything. God, I feel really bad for all he's been through. I hope we can be good friends. I think I could, you know, help him."

"You're a sweet girl," said Kyle. "I think you'll be really good for Jed, too." He smiled at me. His expression revealed such gentleness, and

45

his eyes seemed to sparkle under the drops of seawater that still clung to his eyelashes. He looked beautiful. I wanted to tell him how good he made me feel. I wanted to touch him.

"What?" he asked, smiling curiously.

"I didn't say anything," I said.

"No, it was the weird expression on your face, like you were in a dream or something. What were you thinking?"

"Oh nothing," I laughed, embarrassed. After a moment, I said, "Tell me about you."

"What about me?"

"I don't know really," I lied. "I just feel like I don't really know much about you." What I really wanted to know was if he had a girlfriend.

"What you see is what you get." He shrugged. "Kyle Adams, a Florida boy born and raised, soon to be a US soldier. That's about it."

"Okay, soldier boy, so what are your hopes and dreams?" I probed.

He looked away from me and out to sea. For a while, he didn't answer me, and then he shrugged again. "I'm a simple guy, Rachel. I just want to be a good soldier, marry a pretty girl, and raise a couple of kids. I just want to do my part, that's all."

"Well, that's admirable," I said. I paused, daring myself to ask more. "Do you have the pretty girl in mind?"

"What?" He looked puzzled.

"You know, a pretty girl to marry."

Kyle smiled. "Maybe," he said. "I've been going with this girl for quite a while, but she's in California for the summer, visiting her dad. I might marry her."

The disappointment rushed over me like a wave. The feeling of disillusionment was consuming, and I suddenly felt like there wasn't quite enough oxygen in the air. Kyle must have sensed what I was feeling because his facial expression suddenly changed, and he appeared concerned. "Listen, Rachel," he said, "you're a sweet kid,

46

and very cute, too, but you're too young for me. I thought you got that."

"I know," I said, feeling flustered and foolish, "it's just that I was really starting to like you, and I thought maybe my age didn't matter."

Kyle put his hands on my shoulders and grinned. "Babe, trust me, if you were a couple years older, I'd be all over you. Now"—he winked—"watch out." He dove under the water. I screamed as I felt him grab me around my waist from behind. He lifted me out of the water and tossed me forward. I came down with a splash, and sank beneath the gentle waves. As the water enveloped me, I acknowledged my regret about Kyle, but I hadn't given up hope. *This summer*, I thought, *is full of potential.*

After a while, Jed and the others joined us in the sea. We splashed and teased each other, and we laughed a lot. Even Jed seemed happy.

I remained disappointed about the existence of Kyle's girlfriend. But never before had I felt so included, and to be a part of this group of cool young people was a reality I had never imagined could actually be my own.

I wished the afternoon would never end. But inevitably the sun began to fade from a blinding yellow to a deep orange as it slowly approached the horizon. Hunter had returned from his wanderings, and fortunately it seemed that both he and Jed seemed to have forgotten the earlier fight.

As the sun set, we piled back into the little truck and headed back to Dunedin. The evening glowed, the sky on fire with pink and orange. I knew my grandparents would be starting to worry. After arriving at Jed's house, I reluctantly took my bicycle and headed home. As I rode through the little neighborhoods where children played in the streets and elderly folks strolled slowly, I felt completely content. I smiled, imagining what more this summer held in store for me.

Chapter 4

The hot summer days slipped effortlessly into night, each evening painting a glorious picture of pink, purple, and orange across the sky. I spent most of my time with the boys and their friends, although, much to my disappointment, Kyle often had to work. It used to make me crazy that he had to work so much. Though I really enjoyed Jed's company, I was consumed by my attraction to Kyle. Each time he smiled at me, showing all those perfectly straight, white teeth, I was captivated, mesmerized. There was something about his tanned face and blond hair that was still so boyish and charming. And yet just knowing he was almost a man, and a soldier, made me see him as so much more than just a really good-looking kid. Just the thought of him would leave me light-headed, and though I knew he was out of my reach, I couldn't help but dream of how it would feel to be with him.

The thing was that although Kyle had made clear all the reasons why a relationship between us was impossible, when we were all together I had the oddest feeling that he was watching me. There was something in the way he looked at me, with just a hint of a smile on his face, that warmed me from head to toe. Occasionally, when he looked at me that way, I would catch his eyes and we would find ourselves staring at each other for just a split second before he would look away, appearing almost embarrassed. At those times, I so wished I could tell what he was thinking. There was a part of me that wanted to believe that he was just as attracted to me as I was to him. But then the ever-present reality of the steady girlfriend in California, and the age difference between Kyle and me, would knock the wind out of me, and I would have to admit I was likely just deluding myself. Still, at times I did wonder if Kyle worked so much just to avoid being near me. Whatever the reason, I ended up spending much more time with Jed than with Kyle.

It wasn't long before I started spending so much time with Jed that I barely had time to write anymore. In the past, this would have tormented me terribly, for writing had been my greatest comfort. And yet, as each summer day melted away like chocolate in my mouth, I felt more content than the day before. The days were long and lazy and seemed to complement the friendship that was developing between Jed and me, and though I couldn't deny my infatuation with Kyle, each day I found myself looking forward more than I had the day before to just hanging out with Jed.

Talking to Jed was so easy. I never felt embarrassed or awkward. With Jed I could just be myself. And he was the most honest person I had ever met. It was true that sometimes he got moody, but he always said what he thought, and I never doubted he was telling me the truth.

He told me all about how bad he had felt after his mother was killed, and how angry he had been. He had blamed everyone for what had happened to her. He blamed himself, his mother, his dead

50

father, his grandparents, the president of the United States, the Iraqi people, the terrorists, the army, just everyone. He was so full of rage, he said he wanted someone to hold responsible just so that he could hate them. But really there was no one person to hate, and there was nothing he could do about it anyway. That's when he really got into his music more than ever. He said that when he was listening to music, and playing music, was the only time he didn't hurt.

After Jed's mother died, he had continued to live with her parents for a while. But then, a few months ago, his grandmother had had a heart attack. Jed explained that he had long been concerned about her health. She was at least a hundred pounds overweight, and she smoked all the time. He told me he was always trying to persuade her to live a more healthy life, but she wouldn't listen. She died in the hospital from complications. After she died, social services decided his grandfather was not capable of caring for him and that's when he was sent to live with Rosa.

When Jed talked about his life, he never complained or felt sorry for himself. That was the amazing thing about Jed; he just told it how it was, honestly. But he wasn't only the most honest person that I had ever met, he also listened better than anyone I had ever known before. It was like he really cared about whatever I said to him. He almost never interrupted me, and he would watch me as I spoke, his dark eyes barely blinking as he studied me. It was as if he really was trying to understand everything I said to him.

But I never felt any pressure just to make conversation for the sake of it, and sometimes we just didn't talk at all. We were just as comfortable with each other in our silence as were in deep conversation. And it was one such afternoon when time was slipping silently by as Jed and I strolled together through the trails of Hammock Park that my relationship with him began to morph into something new. It was hot and muggy that day, and the tree canopy provided minimal relief from the sun's unforgiving rays.

51

"Let's see if we can't find somewhere cooler to hang out," suggested Jed, breaking the peaceful silence between us. "It's just too freaking hot here."

"Okay," I answered as I followed him down a shadier trail. "You seem to know this park like the back of your hand. How long have you lived here in Dunedin anyway?" I asked.

"Only about four months," Jed replied.

"It hasn't really been very long then," I said. "How has it been for you, you know, so much change and everything?"

"It's getting better," he said. "I really miss my grandma and grandpa, but Rosa's cool now that I'm getting to know her." He shrugged his shoulders, and we walked without speaking for a while. "Florida's okay, I guess," he continued. "And Kyle, well, he's a good friend. He's kind of like a brother." The trail had taken us to a small wooden bridge that crossed the creek. Jed stopped and leaned back on the rail. "It's much better since you arrived. You're the best thing about this place." He looked at me with those dark eyes that seemed to penetrate me, and I found myself feeling pleasantly light-headed and almost giddy.

"I'm having a great summer since I met you guys, too," I said. "You and Kyle, Tyler and Brook—maybe not Hunter so much— but you guys, you're probably the best friends I've ever had."

"Yeah, they're cool." Jed paused as if he had been about to say something else, but changed his mind. He looked away from me and continued. "But you're special, Rachel. I mean you're special to me. I really care about you more than just a friend." He turned to face me again, and as he looked into my eyes, I knew he was searching my face for a clue. He had exposed himself with his frank honesty, and now he was waiting for my response, and at that moment he seemed so vulnerable.

In all honesty, I did care for him, too. I had found myself thinking of him when I wasn't with him, and I had often imagined how it would feel to be embraced by him and to be kissed by him.

52

But I still had strong feelings for Kyle, and truthfully I hadn't given up hope that he might change his mind about my being too young for him.

"Jed," I hesitated, not really sure what I was going to say to him. "I really like you, but I like Kyle, too. I know he says I'm too young for him, but I really think maybe he likes me."

Jed turned away from me and leaned over the rail of the little bridge. For a moment, he didn't say anything, and I began to worry that he was mad, or worse still, upset. "I don't believe Kyle's right for you, Rachel," he said without looking at me. "Besides, he already has a girlfriend." He turned around, and the expression on his face was one of complete certainty, with no hint of shame or apology. "I know I'm right for you, and I know we're supposed to be together one day. Maybe you think I'm too young to feel like this, but I know how I feel, and the only thing that scares me about that is that you won't realize when you feel the same way about me."

I stood before Jed completely dumbfounded. Not in my wildest dreams would I have anticipated that Jed would proclaim such feelings toward me. For one thing, he was only fourteen years old, and never before had I seen anyone that young so willing to reveal so much of himself, without any regard for how others would respond to that revelation.

"I...I don't know what to say," I stuttered.

"That's okay." He paused. "Look, don't worry about it, all right? Come on, let's get out of here. It's just too freaking hot today."

But I didn't feel like it was all right at all. I felt like I owed Jed an explanation. I felt like we needed to talk and figure things out. The problem was I was so unprepared for what I had just heard, and I didn't know how I felt. I was overwhelmed with emotion.

"Come on," Jed said, smiling. "It'll be fine." He started walking away from me. Lost for words, I followed him, and we walked silently through the winding paths of Hammock Park. The sweat dripped down my back, and my mouth was as dry as if I had swallowed sand. Jed turned to me and looked into my eyes. Always, when he looked at me that way, I felt as if he could see into my heart. "We'll be home soon where it's cool," he said reassuringly, "and you'll be able to get a cold drink. You'll feel better then." It amazed me how he always seemed to know what I was feeling. "All right?" he asked.

"Yeah, okay," I replied.

Chapter 5

For Jed's fifteenth birthday, Rosa threw a party. Of course Kyle and the others were all invited, as well as Kyle's mother and some of Jed's and Rosa's friends from the guitar shop. Jed had brought his new guitar home several days earlier, and he took it almost everywhere with him. It was obvious to anyone who heard Jed play how talented he was. In his hands, the guitar came to life and Jed seemed to feel his way through the music he created.

At the party, Jed played with the other musicians as they covered songs new and old. Many of the songs I had never heard before Jed and I had listened to the old vinyl records that belonged to his grandmother. The music was amazing, but it was the old hippies, tapping their feet and working their instruments to grind out the raunchy blues and rock and roll that belonged to the decades of their youth, that fascinated me. When the sound of the Grateful Dead started to fill the room, Rosa shot to her feet and started dancing. She moved her hands in the air like a deranged Arabian dancer, as she sang the words of Jerry Garcia. It was then that I first heard the song "Tennessee Jed."

Eventually Rosa danced herself out of breath and plopped down on the sofa beside me. "What do you think, *chica*, will we make a hippie of you yet?" She smiled, nudging me.

I laughed. "Rosa, I don't know what to think, but I will say that I thought I was a bad dancer until I saw you."

"That's what you call feeling the music, baby," she said, winking. "That's what we Deadheads do."

I shook my head and smiled. I admired Rosa. I had never met anyone like her before. She seemed so independent and free spirited compared to all the adults I had known. And she was beautiful, too, in a way that was natural and unintended. In many ways, Jed was very much like her.

Ever since Jed had shared his feelings with me, I hadn't been able to stop thinking about him. His words that initially had shocked me had created a sensation deep within me that grew each day until I was consumed with warmth and pleasure whenever I remembered them. Yet we never discussed the conversation, and around each other we acted as if nothing had been said.

I turned to Rosa, suddenly curious if she had noticed anything different about Jed. "How do you think Jed's doing?" I asked.

"Tennessee, you mean," she said. "I think he's doing better. He's doing a lot better since you've been around. He sure is crazy for you, little girl, so be gentle."

I blushed. I had not expected Jed's grandma to be so frank with me, and I was even more surprised that she knew how Jed felt about me.

"Did he tell you that?" I asked.

"He doesn't need to tell me, honey. If you open your eyes, there are some things you can just see."

56

There was something about the way that Rosa looked at me that made me a little nervous, and I wasn't at all sure that I wanted to discuss my potential love life right then, so I quickly changed the subject. "Jed told me that when he moved here, he didn't really know you very well. How come?" I asked.

"Well," Rosa said, her expression almost melancholy, "part of the reason, I think, is that Tennessee's other grandparents blamed my son, Tennessee's father, for messing up their daughter's life. After she passed, they didn't really want me to see Jed much at all."

"That's sad," I said. "But you said that was part of the reason. What else happened?" "I'm sorry, what was that?" Rosa appeared distracted and far away.

"You said that was only part of the reason," I reminded her.

"Yes. You see, Tennessee's mother was raised in a military family, and as you know, she died after being injured in the Iraq war."

"So?" I said.

"When I was younger, Rachel, I protested against the Vietnam War. I'm a pacifist. That means I don't believe that going to war is a way to resolve anything. I didn't support the Vietnam War, and I don't support the one in Iraq either. Never have. Tennessee's grandparents never agreed with my opinions or even tried to understand them. They thought of me as unpatriotic and actually offensive, I guess. After they lost their daughter in Iraq, then they really resented me, and anyone else that believes that the U.S. has no business being over in that country." Rosa sighed and shook her head.

Carla, Kyle's mother, approached, carrying a couple of bottles of beer in one hand. She handed one to Rosa. "Sorry, kid," she said, smiling at me, "you're a little too young." She turned to Rosa. "What on earth were you guys just talking about that has you looking so serious?" she asked.

Rosa took a swig of beer before answering. "Iraq," she said.

"Oh," said Carla. "I guess that is serious. Well, I know how you feel about it," she continued, looking at Rosa. "But seeing as my son has signed up, my feeling is that we need to be behind our troops all the way."

"You can support the troops without agreeing with them being in Iraq," argued Rosa.

"I don't think so," said Carla. "I don't think that it's right for us to judge the decisions of the president and the generals during wartime, and I think the soldiers who are serving over there need to know we believe 100 percent in what they're doing."

"But aren't you scared?" I asked.

"Of course I'm scared. I pray to God every day that if Kyle goes there he'll keep his head low and be fine. But we need boys, and girls for that matter, who are willing to serve the country and lay their lives on the line for what's right and what America stands for. Besides, the military is a great way for a young person to develop into a responsible member of society who can think on their feet."

"I don't agree with that either," interrupted Rosa. "I believe that in the military kids are taught how *not* to think for themselves. They are told not to question orders but to do what they're told to do, whether it's the right thing or the wrong thing."

"But we all have to follow orders sometimes," protested Carla. "Society has rules, you know."

"True," agreed Rosa, "but there are some rules that need to be broken and some orders that need to be ignored."

"Well, if that's what you believe," said Carla, shrugging.

"It is," answered Rosa. There was a pause in the conversation, and I began to feel concerned these longtime friends were genuinely fighting with each other.

"You must have been a very difficult child," said Carla.

"You bet I was, honey," said Rosa, chuckling. She raised the bottle of beer to Carla. "Cheers."

"Cheers," replied Carla, and the bottles clinked musically as they collided.

Chapter 6

The more I considered Jed's confession of his affection for me, the stronger my feelings for him became, and I wanted so much to tell him how I felt. Every day, I would start the morning with the intention of doing so. But whenever I saw him, all my courage would dissipate, and I'd find myself feeling squeezed, unable to fully expand my lungs as my breath stuck in my throat. Each evening after we'd parted, I'd find myself reciting the same speech I had wanted to say to him but had not. And at night, before I slept, I'd write in my journal of all the emotions I was incapable of revealing. I felt the summer slipping between my fingers like the hot, dry sand of these beaches that I loved. What will it take, I wondered, for me to finally share my feelings with this boy who had by now become an integral part of my very existence?

59

Early one morning, Jed and I rode our bikes to Honeymoon Island. This was one of our favorite places to just spend time together. Honeymoon Island was a Florida state park within the city of Dunedin, so it was protected from the commercial development that had already befallen much of Florida's coastline. The beaches were unspoiled, and the vegetation lush and wild. On a typical weekday morning, it was easy to find an area of beach that was entirely secluded, and on this particular morning, we were not disappointed. The sun was already high and hot when we arrived, already sweaty from the ride. We laid our bikes in the sand and placed the towels and small coolers we had brought in the shade of a tree. "Come on," yelled Jed as he began pulling off his shirt, "I'll race you to the sea." He began bounding toward the water as I began stripping down to the bikini I wore beneath my clothes. "How is it?" I called.

"Hurry up and join me and you'll find out," he yelled back. I walked casually toward the gentle waves that rolled repeatedly toward me, beckoning me. Each soft wave seemed to release a little sigh of relief as it spilled onto the warm beach and was absorbed into the sand.

As I moved through the water, I felt the warm liquid ascending around my thighs. I curled my toes into the sand, caressing the soft, doughy texture of the seafloor. A few feet from me, Jed dove under water and began to swim toward me. I dipped under the water, too, to wet my hair and wash the morning's sweat and grime from my face. When I emerged from the water, Jed was standing close by me, his dark eyes watching me as drops of seawater fell from his black mane of wet hair and ran down his caramel skin. I wanted to reach out and touch his skin, his face, his chest. I wanted to tell him that when I was with him I felt safe and that he made me happier than I had ever felt before. My heart pounded as I tried to speak, but the words would not come. And so we just stood there, close together, as the warm water surrounded us in its vast embrace.

After a while, Jed turned to face the beach, and his eyes appeared to explore the scenery. He sighed deeply. I waited for him to speak. "You know, I used to come to this place a lot after I first moved here," he said. I remained silent. I sensed he wanted to tell me something, and I didn't want to interrupt him. For a long while, he said nothing, and then he looked down at the water and continued. "When I first got here, I felt like I would never feel okay again." He raised his eyes to look at me. "And there was nobody I felt like I could talk to. So I used to come here so I could be alone with no one to bother me. I used to just sit out here and think about everything that had happened."

"It must have been very hard for you," I said. "I can't imagine how terrible you must have felt with how everything turned out."

Jed turned and looked out to sea. "Sometimes, I would imagine that I would just start swimming out there until I got so tired I just couldn't swim anymore. And then I would just drown. I'd sink underwater and the sea would fill my lungs, and I wouldn't have to think about the things I'd lost anymore."

"I'm sorry, Tennessee," I said. I had never called him by his first name before, but somehow it made me feel more connected to him at that moment. I wanted to say more to comfort him. I wanted to wrap my arms around him and lay his head on my chest and tell him that everything would be okay, but I was petrified. I swallowed hard, searching for the right words. But Jed continued before I knew what to say.

"You know, my grandma has a gun she keeps next to her bed."

"Really?" I interrupted. I was surprised. I never pictured Rosa as the type to keep firearms in the home.

"Yeah," he answered. "My father gave it to her when he left to marry my mom. He said he wanted her to have it so she would be safe on her own. That's why she keeps it, because he gave it to her." Jed shook his head, and again he sighed. "Once I took it." He paused, and I held my breath, somehow afraid to make a sound. "I took it from her nightstand and brought it out here. I put it in my mouth, and I was going to pull the trigger."

"Bloody hell, Tennessee, why?" I was alarmed and horrified by his confession.

"I don't know. I just wanted everything to stop. I wanted to stop feeling."

"What stopped you from doing it?"

"I thought about my grandpa and how he had already lost a daughter and his wife. And I thought about Rosa, too, and how she had lost her only son. I didn't want them to suffer any more. I don't know, but something just stopped me."

"Well, thank God," I said, feeling shocked and dismayed and yet also relieved. "Thank God," I repeated in a whisper, more to myself than anybody else.

Without a word, Jed moved toward me until his body was only inches from mine. His arms wrapped around me, and as I embraced him, I felt his lean body trembling. Our eyes locked as I raised my gaze to meet his. The sadness on his face melted away as he smiled almost imperceptibly, just barely shaking his head. "You are so beautiful," he whispered as he looked deeply into my eyes, "and it's not just the way you look, although to me you're perfect. But it's more who you are inside. You're just a beautiful person."

I knew Jed meant every word he was saying to me, and I was so overwhelmed with emotion that I had to swallow hard just to hold back my tears. Never before had I felt so needed and cared for by someone. It was something that I had secretly longed for, for as long as I could remember. "I don't know what to say," I said, as I looked down, feeling suddenly shy.

"You don't have to say anything," he said.

As I raised my face to him, he lowered his toward mine. Our noses bumped and he chuckled softly. "Let's try that again," he whispered, and I could feel his warm breath against my lips. He turned his head ever so slightly to one side, and I saw him close his eyes just a split second before his lips touched mine. As I lost myself in the softness of his mouth, I realized my eyes had closed, too. We stayed there, holding each other closely, blanketed in the soft warmth of the sea, for what seemed like hours. But as the blazing sun moved across the sky, even our embrace could not distract us from our need for hydration and nourishment. As we strolled hand in hand toward the shore, I tried to recall if I had ever felt so happy before.

We laid our beach towels side by side in the shade of a palm tree, and there we sat, enjoying cold soda and the tranquility of our very own private beach paradise. After a few minutes, we laid down facing each other. Jed raised his hand to my face and stroked my cheek. "Thank you," he whispered. "Thank you for coming here. I don't just mean here to the beach today. I mean thank you for finding me. I don't know what I might have done if I hadn't met you." I held my breath, remembering how he had almost killed himself, right here on this beach. I tried to think of the right words to say, but they wouldn't come. "I need you, Rachel," he said. "I really mean it. I even think I might love you."

I wrapped my arms tightly around him, somehow knowing that right then he needed me to comfort him. "We're really good together, aren't we?" I said. "Everything is going to be okay, you know." As I held him close to me, I felt all the emotion finally releasing from my body, and a sense of peacefulness within me that I had never before experienced. "And you know what else?" I whispered. "I feel like I'm starting to love you too."

"I know," I barely heard him say

Chapter 7

After that morning on Honeymoon Island, Jed and I became almost inseparable. As soon as I rose in the morning, I would call him and we would make plans to meet just as soon as we could. We would spend the whole day together, and my grandparents had to set a curfew just to get me home at a reasonable hour.

Even after I arrived home, we would talk on the phone for hours into the night. At times, my grandparents would express concern about how much time I was spending out of the house. But then my grandma would smile at me and tell me how sweet it was that I was so taken with such a nice young man, and that she was happy to see me so cheerful compared with my usual solemn self.

I never felt bored when I was with Jed. We never seemed to run out of things to talk about, and I was able to share so much with him that I had never dared tell anyone else before. When we weren't talking together, he would play his guitar for me and sing songs. I even read him my poems, which I had never done for anybody else.

Together we listened to lots of music. Jed's knowledge of music was so extensive, and he exposed me to such a variety of sounds and bands. For the first time, I began to develop a true appreciation of music.

When we walked together, if we were alone, we held hands. When we were by ourselves in his room, or at one of the parks or beaches, we would sit very close with our arms around each other. When we kissed, the kisses were soft and tender. Each time, I would close my eyes and all my body's energy seemed to focus on the sensation of his mouth pressing against mine. I would feel overwhelmed with pleasure, my awareness of space and time fading as I became consumed by my senses. I would imagine him touching me in ways I had never been touched before, and yet I said nothing, and he did not try. For this I was grateful, for though there was no denying my desires, I felt shy and intimidated by my own inexperience and youth. Whether Jed's restraint resulted from an awareness of this, or whether he felt his own insecurities, I didn't know.

Though Jed and I spent a lot of our time alone together, we also still hung out a lot with Kyle and the others. I still really enjoyed the company of my new friends, and the feeling of being included and belonging. Jed and I were never affectionate with each other in their company, though, because we were both too self-conscious. Nonetheless, they were all quite aware of the romance that had developed between Jed and me, and they often teased us mercilessly. Whenever Jed and I were sitting close together, I would feel Kyle's eyes upon us, observing us. I wasn't sure if he disapproved of our relationship or if he was just amused. But whatever the reason, he always seemed oddly interested in the two of us together.

One bright morning, Jed called me before I was even awake. "Were you up yet?" he asked innocently.

"No," I replied. "Do you know the time? It's barely seven thirty in the morning," I complained.

"Oh, I'm sorry," he said without sounding as if he meant it. "Anyway," he continued, "Kyle's all bummed out. His girlfriend called from California last night and said she wasn't coming back to Florida."

"Really?" I said, intrigued by this unexpected news. "Why?"

"She met someone, another guy. She's been seeing him, I guess. Whatever, but last night she called and broke up with Kyle. He's totally pissed and really broken up about it."

"Oh, that's terrible," I said, with genuine sympathy for Kyle. I knew how much he cared for this girl, and that he had anticipated a future with her. As soon as I had spoken, however, I felt a pang of guilt as I recalled how much I had initially resented her for that very reason. Worse still was that there was a part of me that was happy she was not coming back, even though I no longer wanted to be with Kyle. "But still," I said, as I tried to clear the disquieting thoughts from mind, "why did you call me so early? Not just to tell me that?"

"No," he replied. "Last night, when Kyle was so upset, I guess his mom called his dad to talk to him, and this is the part that I called you about—Kyle's dad said he could take out his boat today. I guess he figured it would cheer him up or something. Anyway, it's good for us, right? Kyle said he was going to take it out to one of the islands and that we could hang out with him. And I checked the weather, and it's going to be a great day on the water." Jed sounded really excited.

"Sounds like fun," I said. "What time?"

"He said about eleven. I changed my guitar lesson to early this morning so we could go. So after the lesson I'll just swing by your house on my board, and then we can hoof it down to my place and meet them."

I was excited. I had never been out on a boat on the Gulf before. But I had often seen groups of young, happy, attractive

67

people zipping along the channel between the Dunedin coastline and Clearwater Beach. Their motorboats would bounce off the wakes of other boats, as they seemed to fly across the sparkling sea. The boats' engines roared, while the passengers held on tightly to the rails with one hand and beers with the other. And pretty girls would laugh hysterically as their boats jumped higher and higher from the waves, their colorful bikinis bouncing with each impact. I had imagined many times how it would feel to be one of them out there on the water. Today, I thought, I would finally have my chance to find out.

After hanging up the phone, I quickly got up to shower. I was full of anticipation as I started to think about what I would wear. It surprised me how much I wanted to look really good out there on the boat. In my room, I finished drying myself off. I tossed the towel on the bed and turned my naked body to face the full-length mirror that was attached to the door. In many ways, I had tended to avoid looking at my body ever since I had entered puberty. It wasn't that I was embarrassed about the physical changes that I had gone through; it was just that those changes had resulted in my body seeming almost foreign to me. For a long time, I felt so unfamiliar with my physical maturity that the sight of myself made me feel as if I were looking at a stranger. But now I wanted to really look at my physical self. I no longer felt like a girl child in a woman's body. My eyes explored my reflection in the mirror before me, as I really considered my female form for the first time. I pondered the sight of my breasts, the curve of my waist and the hair on my body. As I gazed at myself, I sensed my own sexuality. I stood as if at attention, like a soldier standing for inspection. I held my head high and my shoulders back as I tightened my abdomen and brought my legs firmly together. I felt surprised by how strong and yet feminine my body appeared. I acknowledged that I was not very tall, and I thought my boobs certainly had room to grow. I frowned, wishing that my legs were longer. But I was slim and my curves all seemed to be more or less in the right places. For the first time in my life, I really recognized my own

68

sexual attractiveness, and I suddenly felt both delighted and apprehensive.

The newly discovered awareness of my physical self was surprisingly arousing, and the excitement I felt as I prepared to spend the day with Jed and the others escalated. As I modeled my lime green bikini with pink polka dots before the mirror, I threw my hips sideways at tantalizing angles as I tossed my long, wet hair from side to side. All the while, I thought of Jed, and how he would feel about me when he saw me. But my thoughts also turned to Kyle, and even Hunter and Tyler, and I wondered if they, too, would notice me and my young womanhood.

Chapter 8

When Jed arrived, guitar on his back and skateboard in hand, I was ready. I had left my blond hair to dry loose and naturally. I wore my bikini beneath cutoff blue jeans which I had cut shorter than they had previously been. On top I wore a sleeveless buttonup shirt that I had left open except for tying it around my waist, and so revealing the skin between my navel and the top of my low riders. I had considered makeup, but by this time in the summer I had a natural tan, and I had decided I didn't need it. Besides, I didn't really know how to apply makeup and I was worried I'd make myself look stupid instead of sexy.

When I opened the front door to Jed, he looked pleasantly surprised. He took both my hands as he looked at me and grinned. "Wow!" he said. "You look different. I mean, you look great, it's just that I've never seen you dressed like that before." He pulled me close to him and hugged me, his hands touching my bare waist. "I missed you since last night," he said.

"Me too," I responded. He let me go and smiled at me.

"Are you ready?" he asked. "We're going to have a great day, so the sooner we get there the better."

"Let's go," I said. I yelled good-bye to my grandparents and slipped my hand into Jed's as we left.

When we arrived at Kyle's house, everyone was already there waiting for us. Immediately on our arrival, I noticed Hunter looking at me, or, more specifically, at my body. I could see by his facial expression that he liked what he saw, and he did not try to hide his appreciation. After staring at me, he raised his eyes to meet mine and winked at me, a bare hint of a smile on his face. "Looking good there, Rachel," he said. Although I felt flattered by his attention, I also felt apprehensive. Something about the way he looked at me made me feel uncomfortable and self-conscious. I looked away from Hunter and toward Jed. Jed was watching Hunter, and I could see in his eyes that he did not appreciate Hunter's interest in me.

I noticed Kyle did not look as cheerful as usual, and I remembered about him breaking up with his girlfriend. He saw me watching him and he smiled a melancholy smile. "Hey, Rachel," he said. "You look cute today."

"Thanks," I said. "I'm sorry about your girl."

"Me too," he said. "I can't believe she was cheating on me." He shook his head sadly. "Anyway," he said, shrugging, "I figure it's her loss. I can do better than her."

"You bet you can," said Brook as she walked over to Kyle and put her arm around him. "You know we women can't resist a soldier, especially one as fine as you." She squeezed his shoulder. "Exactly my thoughts," responded Kyle. "Thanks, Brook. Come on, everyone," he continued, as he began walking toward his truck, "let's get going before we lose half the day. It's going to be tight in the truck with all the stuff back there, so we'll have to squeeze some."

"Rachel can sit on my lap if she wants," said Hunter, as he raised his eyebrows suggestively at me. Kyle looked at Hunter with a hint of disapproval.

"No," he said, as he turned his attention to me. "I think it's better if Jed and you ride up front with me. It's not far anyway. The boat's just down at the Dunedin Marina."

It was the perfect day to be out on a boat. The blue sky was interrupted only with wisps of occasional cloud. Sunlight danced on the water, sparkling with flickers of gold. A gentle breeze cooled the usually hot and humid Florida air, and caused the typically still Gulf to be a little livelier than usual. I took a deep breath and smelled the seawater. Jed sat beside me toward the front of the little motorboat. He was shirtless, and the brown skin of his bare arm touched mine. We rocked gently in unison as playful little waves rolled under the vessel.

Brook and Tyler sat together at the back of the boat. Brook had already greased up with sun lotion, her tiny bikini revealing her tanned body. She wore dark sunglasses and she was laying her head back against the rail as if to absorb the sun's rays. Tyler's hand lay casually on Brook's thigh. He appeared relaxed as he sipped a Mountain Dew. He leaned over and whispered something in Brook's ear. He was grinning, and his eyes shifted around to see if anyone was listening. She giggled without raising her head, and I noticed Tyler squeeze her knee affectionately. The boat's engine was already humming. Kyle stood behind the large metal steering wheel. He appeared confident and commanding as he stood there. On the dock, Hunter untied the boat and tossed the rope toward us as he jumped aboard. "Let's rock," he said.

The little boat maneuvered out of the Marina and into the channel. To my right, I could see the waterfront condominiums and mansions of Dunedin. As I looked left, I smiled as I saw the rich vegetation of Honeymoon Island and remembered the time I had spent there with Jed. As soon as he was able, Kyle unleashed the boat's engine. The roar was so loud that communication was only possible if you shouted at the top of your lungs directly into the listener's ear. We began hurtling forward at what felt like a tremendous speed. The wind was wet with droplets of seawater. It blew my hair so chaotically and violently that it whipped my face with stinging lashes. I had to grab it with my free hand and hold it back, and I wished I had tied it up as I usually did.

The boat flew through the channel, bouncing over each wave and landing with a thump on the water. When we passed over the wake of another boat, our little vessel would fly higher out of the water and if I hadn't been holding tightly to the railing, the impact when we landed would have thrown me from my seat. I must admit I was a little scared. The ride was faster, louder, and seemed more dangerous than I had imagined, and yet I was thrilled and excited and I did not want to stop.

We sped along like this for a while, waving occasionally at other boaters as they passed by in the other direction. It was midday and the sun was high in the sky. I could feel the sun's rays penetrating my skin as the heat became uncomfortable. Jed must have sensed what I was feeling as he asked me if I was burning. "I think I am a bit," I answered.

"Here," he said as he handed me his shirt, "wear this. It'll protect you from the sun."

I pulled the T-shirt over my head. "Thanks," I yelled into his ear to be heard above the engine.

"Anytime." He smiled. Then he leaned back a little and closed his eyes, his arms stretched behind him so they lay to each side along the boat rail. I shifted closer to him, and he put his arm around my shoulder and pulled me close. "That feels better," I heard him say without looking at me. I leaned my head against his chest and watched the scenery fly by as the boat bounced and jumped over waves, hurtling us forward.

I don't know how long we were motoring along before Kyle began to slow the boat down. Time at that moment seemed irrelevant, and I believe I would have been happy to spend the whole day just sitting close to Jed. However, at some point, the roar of the boat's engine began to decrease. "I'm going to drop anchor over by that island," Kyle hollered. He steered the boat carefully toward the little palm-tree-covered paradise. "It looks like we've got the whole place to ourselves," he said as he shut down the boat's motor. "Listen, guys, you all hang here and have a good time. I'm just going to walk around by myself for a while.' His face revealed his pain, and I knew he was thinking about his girlfriend. He took a couple of beers from the cooler and turned to Brook and Tyler. "Just keep an eye on those two," he said, indicating Jed and me.

"Sure," said Brook. "Are you going to be okay?" She looked concerned.

"Yeah, don't worry about it." He shrugged. "I just need to get that slut out of my head."

"I know you're upset right now, Kyle," said Brook, her voice steady and firm, "but Julie's my friend, and you can't talk about her like that to me, all right? I know she hurt you, but she's not like that."

"Whatever! You're all the effing same," Kyle hissed under his breath. He turned to Hunter. "Hunter, have a good time, man, but don't drink all the beer before I get back."

"Then you better hurry up, brother," Hunter responded, smiling as he twisted off the top of a beer and raised it to Kyle.

"Yeah, I guess I better," answered Kyle before jumping over the side of the boat and into waist-high water. He didn't look back as he waded toward the island, holding the beers up out of the warm water.

I watched Kyle disappear around the bend as he wandered along the deserted beach. He looked down at the sand as he walked,

75

lifting his head occasionally to take a swig of beer. I could see how much he was hurting, and I began to feel ashamed again, as I recalled how much I had wanted his girlfriend out of the picture. I guess I hadn't really listened to him when he had told me what he wanted in life. He was right. I was just a kid with no real plans for the future before me. I was just beginning to explore the idea of adulthood and where it might take me. He, on the other hand, though only seventeen, thought he had it all figured out, and now he was facing a future that was uncertain. I thought back to when I first met him and how impressed I had been by the concern he had shown for Jed, and also by his certainty about joining the army. But I also recalled his hostility toward me when he had learned of my parents' wealth. I considered that there was a side to Kyle that harbored a lot of anger and resentment, and I worried about how he might respond to how everything had turned out.

Hunter, Tyler, and Brook had already disembarked from the boat and were messing around in the water. Jed looked at me. "What are you thinking about?" he asked.

"I was thinking about Kyle," I answered. "Do you think he's very upset about breaking up?"

"Yeah," said Jed. "But he won't really admit it. He's more pissed that she cheated on him than anything, and that she's not coming back so she can be with this other guy." He paused as if thinking what to say. "Kyle is an awesome guy. But if he thinks you've screwed him, you'd better watch out, because he likes to get even. And, you know, he gets pissed when he thinks things aren't fair. And when he's pissed, you don't want to be near him, trust me."

"Why does he get so mad?" I inquired.

"Who knows? I think it's got to do with his parents," said Jed. "You know his dad's an alcoholic and has never really held a job or anything. His mom and dad fight all the time about money, and I think Kyle blames him for their money problems."

"Well, he lent him the boat. He must appreciate that."

"I guess. I know his dad has tried to have a relationship with him, but Kyle says he's a loser and that he's not even worth the effort."

I sighed as I thought about Kyle's father reaching out to his son and finding himself rejected. "But he should give him a chance at least," I said. "People change sometimes."

Jed looked doubtful. "I don't know. I think his dad has let him down a lot in the past. At some point, you just stop believing. You know what I mean."

I knew exactly what he meant. My parents may have always been able to provide for me financially, but I recalled how, as a small child, I had asked over and over again for them to play with me and spend time with me. I had longed to go to the zoo or park with them or just have them play with me the way I believed other parents played with their kids. But they were always too busy. Eventually, I just stopped asking. "Yeah, I understand," I said.

"Are you guys okay up there?" I heard Brook's voice calling.

"Yeah, do we have to come and hose you down with cold water or what?" Hunter teased. I felt my face flush with embarrassment.

"Maybe you guys should come and hang out with us," Brook added, sounding a little concerned.

Jed looked at me and smiled. "I don't know what they think we're doing up here," he laughed.

I smiled and looked away. "I can only imagine."

"Come on," he continued. "We'd better go meet them before they start bugging out."

I stripped down to my bikini and dropped my clothes, including the shirt that Jed had lent me, in a pile on one of the seats at the back of the boat. I noticed Jed watching me as I undressed. "Do you like my bikini?" I asked innocently.

"Oh yeah," he said enthusiastically. "It looks great on you."

"Thanks," I said, as I climbed up onto the side of the boat and plunged into the warm, aqua-green water. I pushed my wet hair from my face. "Hey," I said greeting Brook and the others as they bathed in the soothing liquid.

"You probably needed to cool off, didn't you?" asked Hunter, suggestively raising his eyebrows and snickering.

"Whatever!" I responded, annoyed and embarrassed. There was a sudden splash beside me. I looked over as Jed emerged from the water.

"Hey, Jed, I think your girlfriend's all hot and bothered. Were you guys getting freaky up there or what?" teased Hunter.

"Shut up, asshole," replied Jed.

"Yeah, come on, give it a rest, man," said Tyler. "Just because you're not getting any doesn't mean you have to harass the kids."

"What the hell do you know?" said Hunter defensively. "I'm getting plenty, and better than the piece of ass you're getting, too."

Hunter looked at Brook contemptuously. Brook's face turned scarlet as she peered at Hunter with disdain.

"Don't pay him any attention, Brook," said Tyler, looking at her and shaking his head. He turned back to Hunter, an expression of disgust on his face. "Don't be such a douche. Just drop it, all right?" Tyler's tone was deadly serious.

"Jesus, lighten up, man," said Hunter, smirking.

"I'm just saying that you need to show a little respect. Can you do that?" Tyler was obviously agitated by the whole conversation.

"Man, you're uptight!" exclaimed Hunter. Tyler was about to argue, but Hunter raised his hand and interrupted. "Okay, sure, whatever you say." Hunter waded toward the boat, clearly annoyed. "I need another beer," he muttered, as he ascended the boat's ladder.

While Hunter sulked in the boat and drank beer, Jed and I hung out with Tyler and Brook. I really enjoyed spending time with them. Brook was sweet to everyone, and she always made an extra effort to include me when we were together. She was like the mother of the group. Tyler, on the other hand, was usually quiet. But when he did speak, more often than not he said something funny.

He was hardly ever serious, which was why it was so surprising to me when he confronted Hunter.

"Thanks for sticking up for me before," Brook said shyly, looking up at Tyler.

"That's okay," he replied, smiling. "You can pay me later."

Brook scrunched up her face in feigned annoyance, and then gently punched Tyler in the shoulder.

"Hey, pick on someone your own size," I heard a voice shouting. I looked up and saw Kyle approaching, the empty beer bottles in one hand.

"It's okay," Tyler yelled back, "I think I can take her."

Kyle waded into the water. His eyes were red, and I wondered if he'd been crying. "So what's happening?" he asked, flashing his white teeth as he grinned too widely for an honest expression.

"We're just hanging," answered Jed. He eyed Kyle carefully, and I knew he was trying to figure out how he was doing.

"Cool," said Kyle, as he approached the boat. "Hey, Hunter, is there any beer left?" he yelled as he climbed the little ladder.

"Maybe," we heard the voice from the boat respond.

Kyle climbed aboard the little boat while the rest of us waited silently in the water. Our eyes shifted from face-to-face as we tried to read each other's thoughts. We all knew that Kyle was hurting over the breakup with his girlfriend, though he was working hard to conceal his pain. I had gathered from my conversation with Jed, as well as my own personal encounters with Kyle, that the boy's behavior could be unpredictable and even hostile when he felt unfairly treated. I'm sure we were all feeling a little nervous to see Kyle acting so weirdly happy, and so we waited tentatively.

"What are you all being so quiet for?" I looked up and saw Kyle climbing back down the ladder, a freshly opened beer in his hand. "If you all are gossiping about me, you'd better quit it or fill me in. And by the way, what the hell did you all do to Hunter to get him so pissed off?"

"Why, what did he say?" asked Tyler.

"I asked him why he was hanging out by himself in the boat, and he said it was better than hanging with losers," explained Kyle.

"He's the loser," said Jed angrily. "He insulted Brook and he embarrassed Rachel and me."

"Why, what were you doing? You better not have been messing around with Rachel on my boat," said Kyle accusingly.

I felt hot with shame. Though I knew we were innocent, somehow I felt as if I had been caught doing something wrong. I looked down at the water, willing myself to find the courage to speak up and defend my own reputation.

Jed appeared hurt and surprised by the sudden attack. "We weren't doing anything," he said indignantly. "And it's none of your business what we do anyway."

Kyle laughed sarcastically. "I'll tell you what, little brother," he said snidely, "on my boat, it is my business." He stared at Jed as if willing him to argue, but Jed just rolled his eyes and looked away. Kyle took a long swig of beer, and turned his gaze toward me. "Anyway, you're an idiot to trust a chick. She'll mess you up every time. Isn't that right, Rachel?"

I looked into Kyle's eyes, searching for something to help me comprehend his cantankerous tone, but his face revealed nothing. His eyes appeared empty, reflecting no emotion. I found myself hesitating, not knowing what to say. What I had to do with his frustration I didn't know, but his contempt toward me at that moment was palpable. I looked at Jed, almost pleading for his help in responding to Kyle's antagonism. Jed looked me straight in the eye and shook his head, and I knew he was warning me not to say anything. For a moment, nobody spoke. The only sound was the sound of the sea gently sloshing against the boat. Then I heard Brook's voice.

"Hey," she said. She looked at Kyle and smiled sympathetically as she waded toward him. She wrapped her arms around him and hugged him closely. "You know I love you, and I know how you're hurting. But you can't take it out on all of us, and I know you don't believe that all girls will let you down, right?" Her tone of voice was soothing and reminded me of a mother comforting a brokenhearted child. She released Kyle and looked up into his eyes. He looked back at her and held her gaze for a long time. His lips began to tremble, and a tear spilled from his eye and trickled down his face. Brook's face softened, expressing her compassion and understanding. She embraced him for a second time, and this time Kyle laid his head on her shoulder. As his shoulders began to shake, I heard him sob. Brook stroked his short hair. "It's okay, baby," I heard her whisper. "You're going to be okay."

Brook held Kyle while he wept. Jed and I said not a word, but I could see from the expression on Jed's face that he was concerned. I could tell that Jed had never seen Kyle cry before, and he was obviously shocked.

After a little while, Kyle appeared to calm himself. He sniffed and lifted his head from Brook's shoulder while he wiped his face with the back of his hand. Tyler approached him and placed a hand on his shoulder. "Are you all right, man?" he asked.

"Yeah," sniffed Kyle. "Yeah, I'm fine. I'm sorry about that." He took a deep breath and blew it out slowly. "I'm sorry, you guys," he continued, looking at Jed and me. "Shit," he shouted as he covered his face with his hand. He seemed embarrassed. He took another deep breath as he folded his arms across his chest and shook his head. "I guess I'm just not dealing that good with all of this. I'm really sorry everybody."

I smiled at him. Although he had been so obnoxious to me just moments earlier, seeing him cry like that, I just couldn't stay angry with him.

"Don't worry about it, man, you don't need to be sorry," said Jed. He shrugged as if to say it was no big deal.

"Yeah," added Brook. "Don't apologize for the way you feel. You were with Julie a long time. Of course it's going to hurt. Don't feel ashamed about that."

"That's true," said Tyler. "You've just got to give it time, man. That's all, just give it time."

"I can't believe you were crying like a baby." Hunter's voice resonated above us. I looked up to see him leaning over the side of the boat and grinning mischievously. "You're such a pussy."

I felt my anxiety level begin to rise again as I anticipated more conflict, this time between Hunter and Kyle. Kyle looked up at his friend out of the corner of his eye. I held my breath and waited for his response. Suddenly Kyle laughed and shook his head in defeat. "You're right," he said. "I am a pussy. But only because of that lying bitch in California."

"There you go, man," said Hunter. "Screw her. There are finer chicks than her that would be more than happy to wrap their legs around you, brother, mark my words."

Brook grunted in disapproval. "You're disgusting," she said, frowning at Hunter.

"Whatever," replied Hunter, "it's true."

"You know there are younger kids here, don't you?" she scolded, as she looked in the direction of Jed and me.

"They're not that young," said Hunter, looking at me. Brook obviously thought better than to continue the conversation, because she rolled her eyes and turned away. Hunter smiled at me, reaching for me with his eyes. I watched him inspect my body, and I felt naked under his gaze. I slipped down into the water, until only my head was not submerged. Hunter licked his lips before turning away from me.

The bright sun was drifting downward to the horizon. Though the afternoon had been somewhat of an emotional rollercoaster, it had been fun. We had eaten sandwiches and chips on the little boat and later played Frisbee on the shore of the tiny island. After the initial argument with Hunter that preceded Kyle's emotional meltdown, the remainder of the day was rather less dramatic. Tyler and Brook wandered off alone for a while "to explore the island." Kyle and Hunter fished without much success, which left Jed and me alone. As always, we found ourselves able to talk freely and without inhibition. We remained mostly in the warm water, our bodies so close as to be almost touching and the fluid between us seemed to physically connect us.

Chapter 9

The day on the boat slipped quietly away. Jed and I grew closer, I felt, with each breath of sea air. But it wasn't only my connection to Jed that seemed to get stronger that day. We all had been present at the moment when Kyle had let down his guard and so openly expressed his feelings. Each of us had been witness to and shared in his pain. Somehow now there was an emotional bond between us, and I felt closer to Kyle and the others than I ever had been previously.

As the pink sun sank steadily behind the little island, pouring new color in ripples across the still glistening water, we all boarded the little vessel for the short journey home.

"Let's get this place cleaned up a little before we leave," said Kyle, as he gathered garbage into a plastic bag. "Whose are these?" he asked, picking up the pile of clothes I had been wearing and had left at the back of the boat.

"The red T-shirt's mine," indicated Jed from the front of the boat. "Toss it over here. I'm going to wear it." As Kyle raised the shirt to throw in Jed's direction, something fell from the shirt's pocket.

From where I stood, the item looked like nothing more than a rolled up piece of paper, but I could see from the expression on Kyle's face it had to be something of more significance.

"What the...," he paused in midsentence as he bent down to retrieve the item. I looked at Jed and saw him watching Kyle anxiously. Kyle held the small white object up to his nose and smelled it. He then raised it above his head so that everyone could see the contraband. His face expressed furious disbelief. "I can't believe you brought drugs onto my boat." Kyle's tone screamed contempt.

"It's just a joint," responded Jed defensively. "It's not like it's freaking crack or something."

"And that's supposed to make it all right, is it?" screamed Kyle. "It's only weed, not crack or coke or something, so no big deal. Is that what you're saying?"

"I'm just saying..." Jed sighed heavily as if exasperated. He appeared flustered and emotionally distraught. For a moment, I was afraid he was going to cry, and I knew he was embarrassed and self-conscious because everyone on the boat was staring at him.

"Weed is illegal and you know it, so don't play dumb with me. You're in some freaking big trouble when we get back home, kid, and if I find out that those dammed hippies at the guitar place are supplying you, I'll make sure you never go back there again, do you understand me?"

"First of all," argued Jed, his voice cracking, "I didn't get it from them. I got it from a kid I know who takes lessons there, too. And second of all, you're not my father, so what's it to you? You have no right to tell me where I can go and what I can do," Jed screamed, shaking with anger and frustration.

"That's true. I'm not your father," Kyle snarled, as he strode angrily toward Jed. "But on this boat, I am in charge. And remember, you don't have a father because he got himself killed smoking this crap." Kyle held up the joint inches from Jed's face.

"You don't know that he crashed because he was smoking," objected Jed, his young face trembling with emotion.

"Well, they found it in his blood and in his car, right? How the hell do you think Rosa's going to feel when I tell her you're messing with this stuff, after what happened to your dad?"

"Don't tell her, please," pleaded Jed. His expression was desperate.

"Oh, I'm going to tell her," said Kyle sternly. "I may not be your father, but I'm the closest thing you've got now, and I think she needs to know so she can keep a closer eye on you. I'm going to tell her because I care what happens to you, whether you understand or not. I only wish my old man had shown even half as much interest in my life."

Jed looked so helpless and sad that I felt my own heart aching for him. "Kyle," I said apprehensively, "maybe you should give him another chance, before you say something."

Kyle turned to face me. He glared at me furiously. I felt so intimidated I had to turn away from him. "Stay out of this," he spat at me. "For all I know, you might be the one who got him into this crap." He shook his head and threw the joint over the side of the boat and into the water.

"That's not true," I said, hurt by the accusation. "I've never done drugs."

"And why should I believe you?" asked Kyle sarcastically, squinting his eyes hatefully in my direction. "You're the one with the money to buy the stuff, and as far as I'm concerned right now, I have no reason to believe anything that you or any other chick says. Why would I trust you?"

I felt as if Kyle had slapped me across my face. I was stunned and crushed by his hostility. I couldn't understand why he was being so brutal to me. I hadn't done anything to provoke such treatment. Deep in by belly, I felt an increasing rage that made me want to vomit. Instead, I found my vision blurring as tears filled my eyes. I turned to Jed for comfort, but he had turned his back to all of us and was leaning over the front of the boat. I turned away from Kyle and the others, swallowing hard as I looked out over the side of the boat. I fought so hard to stop myself from sobbing that my throat hurt, and it was almost hard to breathe through my tightened vocal cords.

"Kyle—" I heard Brook's soothing voice appealing to him, but he cut her off.

"I don't want to hear it right now, Brook," said Kyle, sounding irritated.

"Take it easy, man," Tyler said with an element of concern in his voice.

"I'm telling you guys," responded Kyle through clenched teeth, "it's none of your business. So just stay out of it." Out of the corner of my eye, I saw Hunter subtly raise his hands while he shook his head, indicating to Tyler and Brook to let it go.

"You want to get out of here, Kyle?" Hunter asked.

"Yeah, man, pull up the anchor. Let's go." Kyle started the boat's engine, and its loud hum quieted the deafening silence that had arisen between us. He threw the vessel into gear, and we accelerated quickly to a very high speed. I felt as if we were flying down the channel as we bounced high over the waves and wakes of passing boats. My hair whipped my face and the moist air rushed over me, cooling my skin so that I shivered. I gripped the boat's railing firmly, my knuckles white from the tension. Whereas before I had felt excited by the speed and motion of the ride, now it felt violent and more dangerous. Without Jed by my side, I felt scared and alone. The sun had all but disappeared behind the silhouette of Honeymoon Island to the west, and the sky was turning blood-red. As the light dimmed, the water began to turn a dark gray. I felt a chill through my body, and I was suddenly anxious to be back on land.

Ahead, I saw a larger boat moving toward us quickly. The boat must have been worth many thousands of dollars; it was much bigger and fancier than most I had seen in those channels. As the ship drew closer, I noticed that onboard was a large group of people. Their boat was moving almost as quickly as ours, so they too were holding onto the rails. But unlike us, I could see they were all laughing and smiling and seemed to be having a fun time. As they sped by us, some of them waved and yelled greetings in our direction. I looked at Kyle and saw that he was scowling. "Rich assholes," he yelled at Hunter. "I hope they crash their fancy freaking boat."

The big vessel had produced a large wake, and as we approached, I braced myself for the impact. I wondered why Kyle did not slow down a little. I was sure he knew that hitting the wake would cause us to bounce violently upward.

We hit the wave at great speed. I looked at Jed at the front of the boat, as I felt the vessel leaving the water with sudden upward motion. I closed my eyes and waited for the impact of the landing. The boat came down hard with a thud, and I felt my bones jolted. I opened my eyes and looked in Jed's direction. What I saw shocked me to the core. He was gone. Jed was no longer standing at the front of the boat. I looked around frantically to see if I could see him. He was nowhere, and I knew he had fallen overboard.

"Stop!" I screamed. "*Stop, stop!*"

"What?" shouted Kyle, as he slowed the boat abruptly. "What the hell happened?" He sounded worried.

"Jed, he fell in!" I cried. "He fell into the sea! *Jed! Jed! Tennessee!*" I screamed at the top of my lungs. But Jed was nowhere to be seen. By then I was sobbing, as I looked from east to west for any sign of Jed.

"Oh my God!" shrieked Brook. "Oh my God." She appeared hysterical, and her expression only increased my own terror.

"Where, Rachel? Did you see where he fell in?" demanded Kyle. His eyes revealed his panic, but his tone of voice was authoritative and controlled.

"No," I sobbed, "but it was when the boat jumped the wave back there." I pointed back to where the boat had made the ill-fated leap. I peered into the gray waters in search of the boy who had changed my life. "Please, dear God, let him be okay," I prayed out loud.

Kyle threw the boat into reverse and backed the boat to the approximate spot where Jed had disappeared. It was dusk now, and the near black seas rippled with chaotic colors of dark pink, purple, and crimson, reflecting the sun's decent. Visibility was quite poor, and we strained our eyes, each of us desperately exploring the unforgiving water that had swallowed our friend. My heart was pounding so hard against my sternum that I felt as if I were being repeatedly thumped in the chest with great force.

"Jed!" screamed Kyle. "Shit! Where is he?" he shouted, his hands on his head, his facial expression frantic now.

"Jed! Jed!" we all screamed as we hung on to the boat's rails and peered into the darkening water.

"Look," yelled Brook, "I think there's something in the water right there. I think it's blood." We all ran to where she stood and looked in the direction in which she pointed. It was true. The redness of the water there did not appear to be that of the dying sunlight, but rather a dreadful substance floating there, like a marker in the water.

Instantly, there was a loud splash. In my heightened state of anxiety, it startled me. I jumped and turned to see Kyle hastily swimming toward the foreboding red water. Each stroke of his arms was strong and determined, as he drew ever closer to the blood. He suddenly dove underwater and out of sight. I held my breath as I waited and prayed for him to emerge, my beloved Jed alive in his arms.

I waited, staring at the red sea, unable to look away. I mentally willed Kyle to appear, but to no avail. I felt myself shiver in the warm breeze. "Where is he?" I heard someone hiss under their breath. Kyle had been gone for far too long; something was wrong. My sense of panic grew as I considered the possibility of both Kyle and Jed drowning while we stood watching. Nobody spoke. I don't believe anyone was even breathing.

I saw Tyler grabbing a life jacket. "I'm going in after them," he stated.

"Wait," said Brook, "I think I see someone."

As I watched Kyle emerge from the dark water, I heard myself scream. My screaming quickly softened into quiet sobs, my mind and body not yet sure if I should laugh or cry.

I couldn't yet see if Kyle had found Jed, but I could see from his face that he was frightened and exhausted. He was panting, almost gasping for air, and his skin appeared pale and ghostly against the dark water. He was treading water, his left arm moving back and forth to keep him afloat. I realized he was not using his right hand, and I saw that behind him he was struggling to hold something, or someone, up. "Jed," I whispered, as relief flooded my senses. But the body Kyle held was motionless, lifeless.

"Quick, I need help," shouted Kyle gasping for breath between words. "I can't hold him. I'm drowning out here."

Tyler quickly put on the life jacket he still held in his hand. He picked up another and tossed it to Hunter. "Quick," commanded Tyler. "We've got to help them."

"There are probably sharks in there at this time of day," said Hunter apprehensively. "This is the time when they feed."

"So we're supposed to let them drown?" exclaimed Tyler, as he jumped overboard.

Brook and I both turned to Hunter. "Are you going to help or what?" said Brook, her tone indignant and accusing. Her eyes bulged from their sockets as she stared at Hunter. He

91

reluctantly put on the life jacket and jumped into the dark and dangerous water.

Tyler had already reached Kyle and had taken Jed's lifeless body from him. He began swimming awkwardly toward the boat as he tried to keep Jed's face out of the sea. Kyle also began swimming slowly to the boat, but he struggled with each stroke. Hunter approached Tyler. "Here, give me the kid," commanded Hunter. "I'm way stronger than you. I'll be able to bring him in. You just make sure Kyle's okay."

Tyler appeared relieved as he pushed Jed into Hunter's arms. Hunter grabbed Jed around the chest and began swimming backward with him. Jed was as floppy and as motionless as a rag doll.

As I watched them approaching the boat, I suddenly thought of Rosa. Jed was surely badly injured, if not dead. How could we tell her what had happened? I felt sick to my stomach as I imagined Rosa's reaction if it turned out that Jed had been killed.

I strained my eyes in the dim light, searching for any sign of life from my boy who had barely begun to live. I could see now that blood spilled from Jed's head and covered his face. I was feeling increasingly nauseated, and I had to swallow hard to stop myself from vomiting. I grabbed the rails of the boat and closed my eyes, afraid I was going to faint.

The sound of Hunter shouting my name brought me back to the moment. "Rachel, come and help us." I opened my eyes to see Brook leaning over the boat's ladder. I ran to her side and peered over. Hunter was climbing up the steps, dragging Jed with him. "You guys grab him when you can and pull him up," Hunter instructed. We leaned over as far as we could and each grabbed one of Jed's arms. He was limp, and I found him hard to hold. Hunter took his torso and pushed him up while Brook and I pulled with all our might.

We pulled him over the rail and laid him on his back on the floor of the boat. Blood poured from a large laceration in his scalp and began pooling beside his head. His eyes were rolled backward in their sockets, barely showing the irises. But what I found most alarming was his lips. They were the color of blue ink. As I looked at his broken body, I just knew that he was dead.

I began to cry again. "He's dead, isn't he?" I whispered between sobs, not really wanting an answer.

"He looks dead to me," answered Hunter. In his voice, I could hear the fear. "I don't think he's breathing," he said, shaking his head.

"Move," commanded Brook. "Let me see if he has a pulse." She kneeled beside Jed's body and took his wrist.

"Is he alive?" Kyle asked as he climbed aboard. His voice sounded desperate.

"He's got a pulse," answered Brook, turning to her friend. "But I don't think he's breathing."

"Well, start CPR," screamed Kyle as he fell to his knees beside Jed. "And call 911." He tilted Jed's bloody head back and pinched his nose with one hand while he pulled open his mouth with the other. Then he bent forward and placed his mouth over Jed's, blowing his breath into the body of his young friend. Jed's chest rose as the air entered his lungs.

Brook called 911 and began speaking with a dispatcher. I stood, petrified, unable to move or talk as I watched Kyle blow breath after breath into Jed's lifeless body. Tyler was applying pressure to the head wound as instructed by Brook. Hunter was starting the boat. We were close to the marina and an ambulance was going to meet us.

"Please, please, little brother, don't die on me, don't die on me," cried Kyle between breaths. Tears streamed down his cheeks. He inhaled deeply, ready to blow another breath as he desperately tried to save Jed's young life.

Suddenly Jed's body began to undulate as he began coughing violently. Instantly Kyle rolled him onto his left side as water, blood, and vomit began spewing from Jed's lips. I stood staring, dumbfounded.

"Rachel, wake up and help. Don't just stand there. Grab a shirt or something and wipe that crap out of his mouth," commanded Kyle.

I had a sense of waking up suddenly from a nightmare. Perhaps Jed was going to be okay. I needed to help. I ran and found the shirt that Jed had lent me, the same shirt that had had the joint in the pocket. I kneeled beside Jed and gently wiped the fluids from his mouth. As I did so, he gasped for air and began to breathe, the color returning to his blue lips.

Kyle began sobbing. His sobs were loud and full of relief. "Thank you, God, thank you." He took the towel that Tyler was holding against Jed's scalp and raised it to examine the wound. It continued to bleed profusely, and he reapplied the pressure. He gently pushed Jed's bloody hair from his face. "It's okay, little brother," he whispered. "You're going to be fine, I promise. I'm so sorry. Please forgive me."

I felt my own tears wet against my cheeks and chin as the reality of what had just happened began to sink in. I had believed that Jed was dead, but he was alive, at least for now. I began to realize just how much I needed him, and how much I would lose if I lost him. I had never felt as close to anyone in my life before as I felt to that boy. I had never been able to talk to anybody the way I could talk to him. And when I was with him, I felt as if my whole world was complete and I wanted nothing more. As I kneeled beside him, I took his hand in mine and held it to my heart.

"He is going to be okay, right?" I asked Kyle, my eyes still blurry with tears, my words pleading. Kyle didn't look at me as he answered. He shook his head sadly.

"I don't know, Rachel," he said, the doubt apparent in his voice.

"But he's breathing on his own now," I argued in desperation. I just wanted him to promise me that Jed would be fine. *Just tell me my Tennessee will be okay.*

"I know he's breathing, and that's good, but he's still unconscious. His brain may be damaged for all we know."

"But you think he's going to be fine, right?" I insisted.

94

"How would I know?" he snapped. "I'm not a doctor." He looked up at Hunter. "Godammit!" he yelled. "Are we there yet?"

"Yeah, we're pulling in right now," replied Hunter.

"Thank freaking God!" Kyle sighed.

As we pulled into the marina, the EMTs were waiting on the dock. At the end of the pier, I saw the blue and red lights of the ambulance and fire truck flashing and swirling chaotically against a backdrop of evening sky. Curious onlookers appeared to strain their eyes as they stared from the pier and the waterfront restaurant beside it. At that moment, the scene seemed surreal to me, and I imagined for an instant that I might be dreaming.

But then reality gripped me again as I heard orders being grunted in gruff voices. "Stand back please, miss," I heard one say, as the EMTs boarded the boat. They brought with them a stretcher and bags of plastic tubes, fluid, and needles, equipment intended to try to save the life of someone who was dying.

One man stood with a pen and paper, asking questions about Jed and what had happened. "Do you know how long he wasn't breathing?" he asked.

"No," said Kyle. "A long time. He looked blue."

The other EMTs were already at work on Jed. They had secured his neck in a hard collar, and he had been placed on a backboard. A lady taped an IV into place and attached a tube which led to a bag of clear fluid. She held the bag above Jed's limp body. Another EMT bandaged his head wound.

"All right," said the technician at Jed's head. "We're ready, let's go." The man who had been taking notes laid his papers at the end of the stretcher while the other EMTs secured the straps that were wrapped around Jed's body. Except for the slight movement of his chest as he breathed, he was completely still.

I suddenly felt a sense of extreme panic as the men lifted the stretcher. They were taking him away. They were taking my beloved boy from me, to a hospital, a place where life or death was determined.

What if they determined he wasn't okay? What if this was to be the last time I saw him alive? I wanted to go with him. I ran to the lady who held the bag of fluid that flowed into Jed's veins. "Can I go with him?" I pleaded.

"Are you related to him?" she asked.

"No, he's my boyfriend."

"I'm sorry, honey," she responded, shaking her head apologetically. "Only relatives, or whoever is responsible for him. Is there anyone here who is responsible for this boy?" she continued, raising her voice.

"I am," answered Kyle.

"Then you need to come with him," the lady said.

Kyle pulled his car keys from his pocket as he followed the EMTs off the boat. He threw them to Hunter. "Make sure you tie the boat properly," he instructed, "and then drive my truck to the hospital." Kyle looked terrified and exhausted.

"Don't worry about it, man," Hunter said. "I've got the situation under control. You just take care of the kid."

"Yeah, please take good care of him," I begged, my voice broken and unsteady through my sobbing.

"Good luck," offered Tyler, but his tone and expression revealed his doubt.

"Yeah, good luck, Kyle," echoed Brook as she attempted to smile, but her face expressed sadness.

Kyle looked away, and I saw him close his eyes. His mouth moved as if he was speaking, but no sound came from him, and I knew he was praying.

—

Brook and I piled into the cab of Kyle's tiny truck. With Hunter in the driver's seat, there was barely room for all of us to breathe. Tyler jumped into the back, and Hunter sped toward the hospital. "Don't get us killed by driving like a maniac," Brook said. Hunter didn't say a word in response, but I saw him looking at her, and his eyes were filled with scorn. She continued, "I wonder if Jed's grandmother knows yet. Hopefully Kyle's been able to reach her so that she can at least be at the hospital if he doesn't make it."

"Don't say that," I screamed furiously, as I turned to look at her. "He's going to be fine, and you shouldn't even think that he's not." But as I spoke these words, I knew I was trying to convince myself more than anyone else.

Hunter pulled the truck into the hospital's parking lot, and we all ran toward the great, red neon sign that crowned the automatic doors that led to the emergency room. When we entered the hospital, Brook took charge, assertively approaching a middle-aged woman who sat behind the front desk. "Excuse me, ma'am, our friend was just brought here in an ambulance. We're here to see him."

The woman looked up at Brook and then turned her head and peered at the rest of us. "Hmm," she grunted, a disapproving look on her face. "What's the name?" she asked impatiently as she began typing on her computer.

"Morales, Jed. Um, no, I mean Tennessee, Tennessee Morales."

The clerk typed in the name and nodded. "Yes, he's here," she confirmed. "You can talk to the triage nurse over there." She cocked her head to one side and looked in the direction of a nurse who sat in a small glass booth beside the door that led back to the treatment rooms. "But I doubt you'll be allowed back there with him," she continued. "They're still working on him." She shook her head as she looked directly at each of us. Her face was completely expressionless, revealing no emotion or clue as to Jed's condition.

"Thank you," said Brook, turning away from the woman. She walked quickly to the triage nurse as we all followed apprehensively. The clerk had been right. The nurse informed us that we needed to wait in the waiting room. She explained that Kyle was back there, and that Rosa had arrived and was also with Jed. She assured us that she would let them know we were waiting. But the nurse refused to tell us anything about how Jed was doing.

We slowly and reluctantly wandered back to the waiting area where we sat without talking. I wept quietly to myself, frequently sniffling as I wiped tears and snot from my face and nose. Brook put her arm around my shoulders and gently pulled me closer to her. I found I was praying over and over to God that Jed would be saved and well. But fear and doubt were suffocating me. I felt as if the air was being squeezed out of my lungs, and I struggled for breath.

It seemed as if we had been waiting for hours, when finally I heard Brook say, "Look, they're coming out." I looked up and saw Kyle and Rosa walking toward us. Rosa's usually bronze skin looked pale, and black eye makeup was streaked down her face. Her eyes were glazed and sorrowful, and she held her hand over her mouth as she shook her head from side to side. Kyle looked almost gray. His eyes were blood-red, and his face was contorted as if in pain.

I jumped from my seat and ran to them, while the others followed behind me. "No," I cried. "Please no, don't say he's dead."

Kyle shook his head as Rosa began to cry. "No, thank God," sighed Kyle. "He's not dead. But he's not good." His bottom lip trembled with emotion.

"Well, what does that mean?" asked Brook, looking first at Kyle and then at Rosa. Rosa sniffed and sighed, wiping the tears from her face with both hands. She took a deep breath and blew it out through pursed lips. "Right now, he has a tube down his throat and a ventilator is helping him to breathe. He has a lot of fluid in his lungs, and he can't get enough oxygen into his blood," she explained. Her voice trembled and cracked with sorrow as she spoke.

"Is he awake?" interrupted Brook.

"No," said Kyle. "He's still unconscious. He has a very bad cut on his head, too, but they did a cat scan and they didn't see any brain damage."

"Well, that's good, then, isn't it?" I pleaded. "I mean he should be fine, right?"

"They don't know yet, Rachel," said Rosa, sadly shaking her head. "He's going to be transferred to the children's hospital where he can be monitored in the ICU. We don't really know how long he went without oxygen. His brain could still have been damaged. We'll just have to wait and see now." Rosa hesitated. "I have to get back to him. They're sending a team by ambulance to get him, and they could arrive at any minute. I need to be ready to go. You all go home now and pray for my grandson." Her face crumpled with emotion as her tears began to fall again.

Kyle grabbed Rosa gently by the shoulders and looked at her. "Rosa," he said, "I can't tell you how sorry I am. I would never hurt him."

"I know that, son," sniffed Rosa, as she looked up at Kyle. She moved closer to him and wrapped her arms around him. "I don't blame you at all," she said. "It was an accident, just a terrible accident."

Chapter 10

For two days, I sat alone in my room with my cell phone in my hand. I wanted so much to be at the hospital just to be near Jed, but he was in the ICU and Rosa was the only one who was allowed to visit with him. And so I just sat and waited, all the while clutching my phone so tightly that my fingers ached. I prayed and prayed for it to ring so that I might hear a voice telling me that Jed was fine. When I could stand it no longer, I would call Rosa, desperately hoping she would share some positive news with me. But every time I called, it was the same. "There's been no change. He's still unconscious."

I couldn't eat; I had no appetite and the very sight of food made me feel nauseated. I couldn't sleep because when I tried, the sight of Jed's blue and bleeding face would appear each time I closed my eyes. If I did sleep at all, I had nightmares in which I relived the accident. Sometimes I would wake in a sweat, having dreamed that Jed was already dead.

My grandparents worried about me. They tried to make me eat, and they grumbled that jeopardizing my own health would not help the boy recover any faster. I begged them to take me to the hospital even though I knew I couldn't see Jed. I just wanted to be nearer to him. But they said it was too far. That was the excuse they gave, although it was my belief that they were afraid. I think knowing that a boy almost my same age lay in the hospital so badly injured, a boy whose company I had been in at the time of his injury, was just more than they could handle.

On the third morning after Jed's accident, I was awakened by Beyonce's voice, which was the ringtone on my cell phone. I had only fallen asleep a short while before receiving the call, and the sound of the phone startled me, rousing me from my dreams where once again I was being tormented by the image of Jed's battered body. It took me several seconds to grasp what was happening. As my thinking became clearer, I reached for the phone. I was about to answer, but then it dawned on me that the call likely meant something had happened. In just a moment, I would hear some news of Jed, but would it be good or bad? I suddenly didn't want to know. I wasn't ready to hear it if the worst had indeed come to pass. I felt my heart begin to pound in my chest as my hands began to shake. I looked at the phone to see who was calling, and, as I had suspected, it was Rosa. I looked at the clock and saw that it was not even seven in the morning. Something very significant must have occurred for her to call me so early. Beyonce's singing continued, demanding that I answer, insisting that I learn the truth about my beloved Jed.

Reluctantly, I opened the phone and held it to my ear. "Hello, Rosa," I said, hearing the fear in my own voice.

"Rachel." Rosa's voice was strong and joyful, and I felt my own heart flutter with relief and elation.

"Tell me," I demanded excitedly.

102

"He's up, Rachel. My Tennessee's awake and talking. In fact, since they took his breathing tube out, I can hardly shut him up," she said, chuckling.

"When? How long has he been awake?" I asked, still not quite believing the good news.

"Oh, his timing was impeccable as usual," Rosa joked. "He decided it was time to wake up at three forty-five this morning. Can you believe him?"

"Oh, Rosa," I said through sobs of happiness, "that's the best news I've ever heard, ever. Thank God. Is he okay?"

"Well," she said, sounding more serious, "the doctors still have to run a bunch of tests on his brain and everything. But I'll tell you what," she said, laughing loudly, "he sure seems fine to me. But why don't you decide for yourself? He's been asking about you all morning."

I felt an overwhelming sense of pleasure and excitement as I anticipated hearing Jed's voice. The idea that he had asked for me during his first hours of consciousness seemed to reach within me and draw me to him. I wanted to crawl right through the phone and touch him. I held my breath, my phone pressed to my ear.

"Rachel," said a very strained and hoarse voice. The voice was so quiet as to be barely audible.

"Tennessee, is that you?" I asked.

"Yes, it's me. How are you?"

"I'm fine now that you seem to be okay," I answered, my tone full of relief. "The question is, how are you? Your voice sounds different." I noticed myself in the mirror as I spoke to him, and saw that for the first time in the last two days, I was smiling. And even though tears streamed down my face, there was color in my cheeks again.

"Yeah," said Jed. "I guess the tube down my throat irritated my vocal cords or something." There was a pause. I waited for him to speak; I was too overwhelmed with emotion at that moment to find the words to express myself. There was so much I needed to say, but I

103

didn't know where to start. "I've missed you, Rachel. Even when I was unconscious, I was dreaming of you. I woke up because of you, because I wanted to be with you again."

His words spilled over me like warm rain washing away all the sadness and fear. I felt rejuvenated, and I was filled with a new sense of passion and purpose.

"I missed you, too," I said, my voice strained with emotion. "I thought you might..." I couldn't finish the sentence. The awfulness of what I had thought was unbearable to me at that moment.

"It's okay, Rachel," said Jed, rescuing me from my own thoughts. "I'm fine. You don't need to worry anymore. But listen, Rosa wants me to rest, and the doctors are in here right now. Maybe you could come down and see me?" I heard the hope in his hoarse and fractured voice.

"I don't know, Jed. My grandparents said they don't want to drive that far." I felt tremendously guilty knowing how disappointed he would be.

"Well, I think Kyle's coming later. I'm sure he can give you a ride." Jed sounded so positive and excited about this prospect that I had to agree.

"Well, okay," I said. "I guess I'll call him."

Jed exhaled a sigh of contentment. "I can't wait to see you," he whispered.

The moment I hung up with Jed, I called Kyle. We arranged for him to pick me up and take me to the hospital with him at around one in the afternoon. At first my grandparents were reluctant to let me go, but after much pleading, I was able persuade them, though they remained concerned. "Make sure that boy drives carefully on the highway," stressed my grandmother. "We certainly don't need any more accidents."

After speaking with Jed and agreeing to visit him, I began fantasizing about how it would be when I finally saw him. Would we cry or laugh? We would hug, I was sure, but perhaps we would kiss each other right there in the hospital room. And how would he look? Would he look ill and pale as he had when I last saw him, or would he once again be the dark and handsome boy I had grown to love? I could only imagine.

Well, regardless of how he looks, I said to myself, *it'll be great just to see him alive. And the one thing I can be certain of is how I look when he sees me.* I picked out my best pair of jeans and the prettiest, pale blue T-shirt I owned. The clothes accentuated my young figure, and I knew they flattered me. I combed my blond hair until it was smooth, and tied it loosely into two pony tails that fell forward on my shoulders. Before this summer I had never considered myself pretty. But now I saw myself differently. The Florida sun had lightened my hair and turned my skin the color of honey. My blue eyes seemed to shine more brightly in contrast to my darker skin. I smiled as I regarded my reflection in the mirror with appreciation. I hoped Jed would like what he saw.

When Kyle arrived to pick me up, he seemed happy to see me. "Are you ready?" he asked, as I closed the front door behind me. He looked at me and smiled. "You look great, by the way. Did you change your hair or something?"

I felt warm with pleasure as I acknowledged the unexpected compliment. "Thanks," I replied, smoothing out my hair with my hands. "I just tied it up differently, that's all."

"Well, you look good, whatever the reason." Kyle grinned widely, revealing white teeth. He pulled his little truck out of the driveway.

The drive to the hospital would take about forty-five minutes, as it was located at the other end of the county in St. Petersburg. For some time, we drove without speaking as Kyle adjusted his radio to the rap station he preferred. He tapped on the steering wheel and nodded his head in time to the music. I had a sense that perhaps he was avoiding talking to me, and I wondered if he was thinking about the accident.

I could feel the tension growing in my chest. I badly wanted to ask Kyle about what had happened on that ugly day on the boat. I could not help feeling that Kyle was at least somewhat responsible for Jed's condition. I felt he had been too harsh on him about the joint that Jed had been carrying that day. And the way he had driven the boat so fast just because he was angry had surely caused Jed to fall overboard. On the other hand, it had been Kyle who had risked his life in order to save Jed's. And Kyle's love and concern for his young neighbor at the time of his injury was obvious to me.

I watched him maneuvering his little truck through the busy streets of Clearwater, his tanned hands planted firmly on the steering wheel, his green eyes shifting their gaze from windshield to rearview mirror as he weaved in and out of traffic. Though I harbored certain feelings of resentment toward him, I still found him extremely attractive. There was something about him that was gritty and raw, and though I could not understand why, it made him all the more desirable to me.

The questions I wanted to ask him played over and over in my head, and I closed my eyes and concentrated, trying to conjure up the courage to confront him.

"Are you all right?" I heard Kyle ask. I opened my eyes to see him looking at me inquisitively.

"I was just thinking," I answered a little uneasily.

"Oh yeah?" He smiled and raised his eyebrows inquisitively.

I smiled back at him nervously and then turned away and looked out the window. I watched the palm trees lining the highway. They appeared to fly by us as we sped toward our destination.

"Well?" said Kyle somewhat impatiently. "Are you going to tell me what you were thinking or what?"

I shifted in my seat and noticed I was biting my lip. "Kyle," I said as I turned to face him. I hesitated, not sure how to proceed with my question. "Kyle," I repeated.

"Spit it out, Rachel, if you've got something to say," commanded Kyle. I sensed the frustration in his tone.

"It doesn't matter," I said, turning away from him. I stared out the window but saw nothing. I was oblivious to the passing world as I pondered my thoughts, furious that I was too much of a coward to speak my mind.

"What," said Kyle, his tone sharp with sarcasm, "you think what happened to Jed is my fault, right?" He did not look at me as he spoke. I could see his hands gripping the steering wheel tightly as his lips curled angrily.

"You don't have any idea what I was going to say, Kyle," I said defensively. "For all you know, it had nothing to do with the accident." But the truth was he was exactly right. He had read my mind perfectly, and now he was calling me on it.

He looked at me doubtfully from the corner of his eyes. "Well then, what *were* you thinking?"

I felt tension grip me, knowing that Kyle had spoken the truth. What could I say? I considered trying to make up something, anything but admit he was right. But in the end, I was too anxious to think clearly, and anyway I thought he needed to hear the truth. "All right," I confessed. "You're right, I was thinking that maybe it was your fault that Jed got hurt. I mean, you didn't have to be so mean to him, and you're the one who was driving the boat." I heard the anger in my own voice as I spoke, and I experienced an odd sense of combined relief and guilt as I spilled the thoughts that had been plaguing me since the accident.

I looked at Kyle, fully expecting him to respond with rage and hostility. Instead, I was surprised to see an expression of deep sadness on his young face. He shook his head slowly, and when he turned to me, I saw his eyes were filled with tears. "Don't you know," he said quietly, "how much I regret everything that happened that day? Do you think that I haven't blamed myself for almost killing him?" Kyle turned his eyes back to the road. His face was tense as he clenched his teeth. I heard him clear his throat and swallow hard. I could see he was struggling to gain control of his emotions. "All my life, the only real family I had was my mom. And then along came Jed, and he had nobody. He was even more screwed than me, and I felt as if he'd been given to me so I could take care of him. I really felt like he was the little brother I never had. So how do you think it feels, Rachel, to see him lying there in the hospital, when I know I was supposed to be protecting him?" He turned to me, his eyes wet with emotion. His expression was humble and resigned. "Rachel, I don't know if you and Jed and Rosa will ever forgive me, but I don't think I will ever be able to forgive myself. So you don't have to tell me it was my fault, because I think about it every day."

Kyle's remorse was genuine, I was sure. And his anguish touched me deeply. The contempt I had felt for him lessened, and I even found myself feeling compassion for him.

"Well," I said. "We've all made mistakes, and I know you would never have hurt him intentionally. Plus, you saved his life. If it weren't for you, he would not be alive." I turned to him and smiled just a little. "Are you going to be okay?"

"Yeah, I guess," he said, shrugging.

I could tell Kyle didn't want to talk about the accident any further, and to be truthful, neither did I. There was nothing left to say. It had happened, and it had been terrible. But fortunately it appeared Jed was going to be fine.

We drove for some time with neither one of us saying a word. Kyle's face had become devoid of emotion, as if he had purposefully put thoughts of Jed and the accident out of his mind. As we drove, I thought about what Kyle had said. He had said that his only real family was his mom, and of course he believed that was true. But it occurred to me that Kyle perhaps didn't realize how lucky he was to have such good friends. I envied him for that. As long as I could remember, I had felt lonely and had secretly longed for a group of friends with whom I could feel close.

When he wasn't in one of his angry moods, Kyle was so charming, and it was obvious that people were naturally drawn to him. Even Hunter, who in my opinion lacked any sense of compassion, seemed to care for Kyle. However, why Kyle enjoyed Hunter's company was a mystery to me. Kyle had a very angry side to him, it was true, but overall he was a decent and caring person. Hunter, on the other hand, seemed to be nothing more than a big, oversexed bully. As I contemplated this strange relationship between Kyle and Hunter, I found myself becoming ever more perplexed, and eventually I was unable to contain my curiosity.

"So how do you know Hunter?" I asked.

"Hmm," responded Kyle as he cocked his head to one side. "That's kind of a long story."

"Well, we have time," I persisted.

"Let me see," he began. "When I was in…let's think here, sixth grade…and so Hunter must have been in eighth grade then. Anyway, he and his mom came to live with us for a while."

"Really?" I said, even more curious than before. "How come?"

"Well, I'll tell you this, Rachel, but you can't tell anyone else, okay?"

"Who would I tell?" I said with a shrug.

"Just promise me."

"Fine then," I said. "I promise."

"All right," he said, sounding satisfied. "Hunter's dad used to abuse Hunter's mom, and Hunter, too."

"What do you mean by abuse them?" I asked as my imagination began to form ugly images.

"You know, he used to beat the crap out of them. Hunter's dad is a really big guy, like Hunter is now. He used to, you know, hurt them bad."

"So how is it they came to live with you?" I asked.

109

"My mom worked with Hunter's mom. When Hunter's mom left his dad, my mom said they could stay with us. So they did."

The traffic in St. Pete was starting to get congested, and we were travelling much more slowly. The unforgiving Florida sunlight poured in through the open passenger-side window from high in the western sky. I could feel my body heating up, and I felt extremely uncomfortable. Under my clothes, my skin was sweating and the dampened fabric was sticking to me, while beneath me the vinyl seat became wet and slippery. I picked up an old auto magazine from the truck floor and began to fan myself. "So is that when you and Hunter became friends?"

"Yeah, I guess so." Kyle looked at me, and I saw that beads of sweat were forming on his forehead and running toward his sparkling green eyes. "In sixth grade, I was still really tiny and a lot of kids picked on me. When I started riding the bus to school with Hunter, nobody messed with me. It was cool for a little kid. I kind of looked up to him, you know? He was big and tough, and he had a reputation for being a hard-ass, so for me it was good."

My throat was dry, and the heat from the surrounding cars and the concrete road seemed to be compressing the little truck. I wished I'd thought to bring a cold drink of water. "Is it much further?" I asked. "I'm really hot and thirsty."

"It's not much further, but it all depends on how fast the traffic moves," he said. He looked from side to side and in the rearview mirror, as if assessing the other vehicles around him. "There's some cold beer in the cooler right here. Get one out and I'll split it with you."

I looked at him apprehensively. "I'm not sure I should drink beer," I said unconvincingly.

"That's fine," said Kyle, shrugging. "But it's all there is to drink in here. It's up to you, but I don't think half a beer's going to affect you too much."

"I guess you're right," I said, feeling a little embarrassed that I had displayed any hesitation. I reached down and opened the plastic

110

cooler. I thrust my hand into the ice and pulled out a can of Budweiser. The metal was very cold and wet in my hand, and I found it to be a welcome relief from the oppressive heat.

Kyle looked over at me, grinning. "Well, go on then," he laughed, "open it."

I felt suddenly awkward and clumsy. Clearly I had reservations about what I was about to do, and yet the concept of sharing a beer with Kyle as we drove alone together in his truck was, on some level, quite appealing to me.

"So?" said Kyle as he watched me. I popped the aluminum ring to open beer and heard the telltale fizz of carbon dioxide escaping. I turned to Kyle and offered him the first swig, but he shook his head. "No, you drink first," he said with a nod in my direction. "You're the one who's complaining about being thirsty."

I raised the can to my lips. I had never tasted beer before, even though the English have always been enthusiastic beer drinkers. I felt the cold liquid on my tongue, and then the prickling of the carbonation. The flavor had none of the sweetness of the sodas I was used to. Actually, I found the flavor quite bland with a hint of bitterness as I swallowed. I considered the beer to be neither pleasant nor distasteful, but the cold relief of my thirst was extremely satisfying. I took a second long swig and then handed it to Kyle.

He raised the can to drink, and I watched him take several large gulps. When he had finished, he sighed. "Now that hits the spot," he said, grinning as he turned to me. "What do you think?"

"It's good," I fibbed.

He handed the drink back to me. "Have some more." I took several long swigs, enjoying the sensation of the ice-cold liquid passing down the middle of my chest and into my waiting stomach. I handed the can back to Kyle and he finished it off in a couple of large gulps. He then squeezed the can with his hand, crushing it, and tossed it to the floor of the truck.

111

"So you were telling me about Hunter," I said, settling back in my seat. I felt better having quenched my thirst, and I was beginning to feel a little more relaxed.

"What about him?"

"Well, how long did he stay with you?" I asked, closing my eyes and enjoying the sun on my face for a moment.

"Just a few weeks," Kyle answered. "His dad said he would get help, and Hunter and his mom went back to him. My mom didn't agree with the decision, and she and Hunter's mom stopped being friends, but Hunter and I stayed buddies."

"Did his dad stop beating him?" I pried.

"I don't know. We never talked about that. Sometimes he came to school with a black eye or a fat lip. I assume his dad did it, but I never asked him. I figured he'd have told me if he wanted me to know."

Chapter 11

Kyle parked the truck in the visitors' lot of the hospital. "Come on," he said. "Are you ready?"

Now that I was there, I didn't feel ready. I felt scared. I had missed Jed so much over the last couple of days. I had thought about him day and night and worried about him until it hurt. I had spent endless hours imagining how it would be when I finally saw him. I had also imagined how it would be if I lost him. But all the wondering and worrying and imagining seemed irrelevant now. "Kyle…I don't know if I can do this."

"What do you mean?" asked Kyle, appearing concerned.

"The last time I saw him, he looked like he was dead. I'm scared. I don't know why, but I'm just so nervous."

"Rachel," said Kyle patiently as he took me gently by the shoulders, "you're going to be fine. Jed's going to be fine, too. Just relax, okay?"

I swallowed hard and took a deep breath. "Okay." We stepped out the truck, and Kyle handed me a breath mint.

"Here, suck this," he said. "We can't go in there smelling like we've been boozing it up together." I took the mint and placed it on my tongue. Kyle smiled at me. "Let's go," he said, taking me by the hand and leading me toward the entrance of the hospital. His hand felt strong and sure holding mine. As we entered the building, I felt a new sense of courage.

When I finally saw Jed, I actually felt a sense of relief. Both of his eyes were blackened, and his head was bandaged. The image of him reminded me of some pictures of wounded soldiers from World War II that I had once seen. But compared to the vision that had been frozen in my mind, the vision of him lying on the boat unconscious and bloody with his skin the color of gray clay, he now appeared more alive than ever.

As Kyle and I walked into his room, an enormous and infectious grin appeared on his face. "You're here," he almost shouted in a hoarse voice as he stated the obvious with palpable enthusiasm.

"We're here," said Kyle in confirmation as he leaned down to embrace Jed. "How are you doing, little brother?"

"Still breathing," said Jed, as his eyes shifted from Kyle's face to mine. "Hey, Rachel," he said, his expression subtly emotional. His dark eyes met mine, and he gazed at me with penetrating tenderness. "Did you miss me?" He smiled.

I grinned and nodded in response. "What do you think?" I said, my heart warm with love and gratitude to have him back as he had been.

"Well, aren't you going to hug me, then?" his said, his tone facetiously indignant.

114

I walked toward him hesitantly. On the other side of Jed's hospital bed sat Rosa. She smiled at me warmly and raised her hand just a little to wave at me. I smiled shyly, acknowledging her greeting.

I felt enormously self-conscious, as if all the eyes in the room were upon me, and yet the power of the emotion I felt at that moment for Jed moved me to him, and into his waiting embrace. I pressed my face into the crook of his neck, and he turned his head toward me so that his full lips brushed my temple and his warm breath moistened my skin. "I'm alive because of you," he whispered.

I'm not sure how long Jed held me in his arms like that. The other people in the room slipped out of my consciousness and there was only Jed and me. I did not feel the need to say anything at that moment, but I had understood what Jed meant. He was alive because he loved me, and that was all that mattered.

The afternoon slipped away in what felt like a heartbeat. As we laughed and talked together, I could feel Jed's eyes upon me, absorbing me constantly. After a while, some people in hospital uniforms came into Jed's room and informed us he had to go for tests.

"We'd better get going anyway," said Kyle. "The traffic could be pretty bad."

"Yeah, okay," I said, rising from my chair. I leaned over Jed and wrapped my arms around his neck. "So if all these tests are fine, you're coming home soon, right?" I asked.

"That's what they say," he said as he embraced me firmly.

"Well then, I'll see you very soon." I untangled myself from his embrace and stood up. Jed looked at me with his large, dark eyes, his expression a little melancholy.

"I'll miss you," he said.

"Yeah, me too," I replied.

—

As Kyle and I began driving back to Dunedin, I was feeling much more relaxed having seen Jed feeling well and in good spirits. Truthfully, I felt so relieved and happy that he was okay, that I myself was almost giddy. Kyle seemed to feel much better too, and as I sat beside him, I realized that I really felt more at ease with him then than I ever had before. Unlike the drive to the hospital, now the conversation between us seemed effortless. Kyle kept joking around with me, and I found myself laughing out loud over and over again. He was so easy to talk to and so much funnier than I had initially recognized. I was pleasantly surprised, too, that Kyle seemed to be enjoying my company just as much as I was enjoying his. I began to feel that something in our relationship had changed. Now, when Kyle talked to me, I felt as if he was addressing me as an equal rather than as a much younger girl. I was enjoying the time alone with him so much that I began to feel disappointed as we drew closer to home. When we arrived in Dunedin, it was already getting dark outside. "Do you need to go home, or can you hang out for a while?" he asked me casually. I looked at my watch. It was only eight o'clock.

"I can hang out," I answered, pleased to postpone returning to my grandparents' house.

Kyle pulled the truck into his driveway. "My mom's working, so we can hang at my house."

"That sounds good."

Kyle followed me to the front door of the house, using both hands to carry the cooler of beer. "It's open," he called after me. I opened the door and held it so that Kyle could enter without having to set the cooler down. I followed in behind him. "Come on," he instructed with a nod of his head. "Let's go to my room."

Kyle set the cooler down by his bed and turned on the large CD player that sat on the floor. The room itself lacked warmth or personality. The walls were eggshell white and mostly bare. There were a couple of beer advertisement posters hanging up. Each one portrayed beautiful, big-breasted young women wearing tiny bikinis and smiling seductively as they held bottles of beer. The furniture in the room was scarce. There was a double bed that was covered with crumpled navy blue linens. Beside the bed sat an old wooden nightstand that was covered with what looked like garbage, such as old car magazines and empty beer cans. A small chest of drawers was located by the far wall, and upon it sat an old TV. Scattered randomly across the beige tiles of the floor were several items of wrinkled clothing and a selection of CDs.

"Sorry about the mess," said Kyle, smoothing out the bed linens and picking up some of the clothes from the floor, tossing them into the closet. He opened the cooler and pulled out two beers. He opened one and handed it to me. "Here," he said. "Make yourself comfortable." He directed me to his bed with a nod of his head.

A steady beat emanated from the CD player and thumped the walls of the small room. I recognized Eminem's voice, as his poetry beat out a song of discontent. I made myself comfortable on the bed, leaning against the wall and hugging my knees to my chest with one arm. I took a long drink from the beer and thought it tasted better this time. Kyle opened his beer and chugged it all down without stopping. After he was done, he belched loudly. "Excuse me." He took another beer from the cooler and then he climbed onto the bed and sat beside me.

I suddenly felt awkward, as if I should say something. But I couldn't think of anything to say. I took another long drink of the beer just to give me something to do. It occurred to me that I had not eaten since the morning. I had heard that drinking on an empty stomach made you get drunk faster, and I wondered if I might be feeling a little woozy already.

"I wonder how Jed's tests went," I said, my thoughts returning the hospital.

"He seemed okay to me," answered Kyle. "Hopefully they're just being thorough and he's fine." The conversation seemed to die abruptly, and I felt we were experiencing one of those so-called awkward silences, except for the flow of words that exploded rhythmically from the CD player as bass tones bounced the room.

"I guess you and Jed have really got a major thing going on, huh?" asked Kyle, looking down into my eyes, his expression one of curiosity.

"You could say that," I answered, feeling a little disconcerted by the question.

He nodded approvingly as he raised his can of beer to his lips and took several large gulps. He swallowed the last gulp loudly and then turned to face me again. "That's good," he said, smiling subtly and with some amusement. "Good for you and Jed."

Something about the way Kyle looked at me, or perhaps the tone of his voice, made me quite self-conscious. It was as if he was implying more in his statement than the words revealed. Feeling a little flustered by the conversation, I chugged down the rest of my beer and began to feel a little buzz that I found quite pleasant.

"You want another?" offered Kyle as he leaned over the side of the bed and opened the cooler.

"Sure," I said without hesitation. Kyle handed me the beer and leaned back against the wall, moving closer to me now so the side of his body was touching mine.

"Can I ask you a personal question, Rachel?" he asked without looking at me.

"You can ask," I said. "But I can't promise I'll answer."

"Well, you don't have to tell me if you don't want to, but let me ask you anyway."

I looked up at him, and my eyes met his.

"What I was wondering," he began, "is have you and Jed...you know, have you guys..."

I anticipated what Kyle was going to ask and was so embarrassed by the thought of the question that I looked away. I took several large swigs of beer.

"Well?" said Kyle. "Have you?"

"Have we what?" I asked, pretending not to know what he was talking about.

"You know what I'm asking, Rachel, you're a big girl. Have you guys ever had sex?" I turned to face him and saw that Kyle was watching me. He expressed absolute seriousness as his green eyes searched mine for an answer.

I shook my head, too humiliated at that moment to find my voice. I felt mortified, but I wasn't sure why. Was it because Kyle had asked such a personal question, or was it because I did not like my answer? Perhaps I wanted to be able to answer yes. Perhaps I wanted Kyle to believe I was no longer a virgin. Maybe, subconsciously, I wished that Jed and I had had sex. It wasn't like I hadn't thought about it many times.

I felt my face on fire, and for a moment I regretted my decision not to go straight home. And yet I found the very subject of the conversation both intriguing and arousing. I nervously sipped my beer and bit my lip self-consciously, as I avoided any eye contact with Kyle.

"I'm sorry if I embarrassed you," said Kyle. He smiled at me affectionately. "It's just that you seem so mature to me recently. I don't really see you as a kid anymore."

I looked up at his face. At that same moment, he was looking down at me, and I realized our faces were very close together. His green eyes were captivating as he gazed deeply at me as if trying to draw me to him. I smelled the aroma of beer and felt the moisture of his breath on my face.

"Um, thank you," I said, unsure of how to respond to Kyle's words.

"You don't have to thank me for anything, Rachel. It's the truth. You are very mature and very attractive, too." Kyle raised his hand and gently stroked my cheek with his fingers. "Whatever your relationship is with Jed, he's a lucky guy." Kyle leaned forward and placed his can of beer on the night stand. "Shall I put that down for you?" he asked, indicating my beer.

"Uh-huh," I almost whispered. He took the can from me and placed it on the nightstand. As he returned to his position beside me, I felt his body even closer to me than it had been before. He smiled at me tenderly.

I could feel my head becoming foggy from the alcohol. My body trembled, and I felt warmth in my chest, abdomen, and pelvis. My mouth was suddenly dry, and I heard the sound of my own heart pounding against my ribs.

Kyle's eyes were penetrating and unwavering as they gazed into my own. I felt transfixed and unable to look away from him. As his fingers slid softly from my face to my neck, I did not object. For a moment, it occurred to me that perhaps I should protest his actions, but I didn't want to. He ran his thumb delicately along my exposed collarbone and then raised my chin with his index finger so that my lips were just inches from his. I felt my own tongue soft against the inside of my lips as I anticipated what I was sure was about to happen. He grinned at me affectionately. "I can't help myself," he whispered. "I have to kiss you." His face moved slowly toward mine, and I closed my eyes and held my breath, waiting to feel his mouth against mine.

Kyle's lips were softer than I could ever have imagined. At first, they barely brushed mine, and then tenderly but firmly he pushed his mouth harder against me so that I felt his tongue and teeth touching mine. As he kissed me, the weight of his body pushed me backward. His arms were wrapped around me, supporting some of the weight. I felt him gently lowering me back and laying me down on his bed. "It's okay," he whispered as he kissed my cheeks, my eyes, and my neck with tiny kisses.

My body was trembling. My breathing had quickened as I reached toward his shoulders and pulled him closer to me. I felt the full weight of his body on me now, as his mouth again explored mine. His hand caressed my shoulder and then my waist. He slipped his hand beneath my shirt, and I felt him caress my abdomen, and then his hand was on my breast. I gripped his body as my own seemed to melt as all the sensations I was feeling for the first time overwhelmed me.

There was a sudden knock at the door that startled me, bringing me instantly back to reality. But almost in the same instant that my brain acknowledged the sound of knocking, Kyle's bedroom door flew open. "What up, bro?" I heard Hunter's voice say before my eyes had time to adjust to the vision of him standing in the doorway looking at Kyle and me lying together.

Kyle quickly pulled his hand from beneath my shirt, but it was too late. Hunter had seen everything. I pushed Kyle off me and sat up, straightening my shirt and smoothing my disheveled hair. I did not make eye contact with Hunter.

Kyle seemed calmer as he resumed a seated position on the edge of his bed, his feet planted on the floor. He leaned forward, resting his elbows on his knees as he looked at the floor. "You could have waited for me to tell you to come in," he said without looking at Hunter. Kyle sounded more upset than annoyed.

"Hey, man, I'm sorry," responded Hunter defensively. "I didn't know I was disturbing anything. I can come back later if you want." For a few seconds he looked straight me as he folded his arms across his chest. Then he shook his head and turned his attention back to Kyle. "What do you think you need, twenty minutes, thirty minutes?"

The shame I felt was almost overwhelming, I felt as if my whole body was burning with embarrassment. *What was I thinking?* I sensed the tears coming to my eyes, but the thought of crying in front of Hunter was so horrible that I fought the moisture back as hard as I could, trying to hide my emotions. I looked at Hunter out of the corner of my eye and saw that he was watching me. On his face he wore a malicious smile that gave me the impression that he knew how humiliated and distraught I was, and that he was enjoying watching me suffer.

"Shut up!" said Kyle, looking at Hunter, obviously angered by his friend's comments.

"I want to go now," I whispered to Kyle, looking down into my fidgety hands as they lay in my lap.

"Yeah," said Kyle as he stood up. "I'll take you now." He reached into his pocket for the truck keys, and I stood to follow him from the room.

"So, Rachel," said Hunter, chuckling, "you couldn't even wait for your boyfriend to get well, huh?"

For a moment, I looked into his mocking eyes as my throat tightened with disdain for him. But was it my hatred for that bully that choked me? No, it wasn't. I resented Hunter because he had spoken the truth. As the boy who had touched my heart was lying in a hospital bed recovering form a near fatal accident, I had been entangled in the arms of his friend, the same boy who was ultimately responsible for Jed's injuries. I felt sick to my stomach as I imagined how Jed would feel if he knew what I had just been doing. Worse yet, what else might have happened if Hunter had not burst in when he did?

Kyle and I did not speak as he drove the short distance from his house to mine. When we arrived outside my grandparent's home, I was still too ashamed to even look at him. "Rachel," said Kyle, almost sternly. He turned his body to face me as he raised my chin with his hand, forcing me to look at him. "It's okay," he reassured me. "First of all, nothing really happened. And don't worry. I'll make sure Hunter doesn't say anything to anyone."

I turned away from him, shaking my head. I was unwilling to forgive either myself or him that easily. That's not true," I argued. "Something did happen, and maybe more would have happened if Hunter hadn't come in. And do you really think you can trust Hunter?"

122

"Look at me, Rachel," said Kyle, but I continued to look away from him. "Please," he urged. Reluctantly, I turned to face him again. He sighed before he spoke. "First of all, nothing more did happen, did it? And second, what Jed doesn't know won't hurt him. Anyway, if it makes you feel any better, I think it was my fault, not yours, and, to answer your question, yes, I do trust Hunter." Now Kyle turned from me. The expression on his face revealed regret. "Look, maybe I shouldn't have kissed you," he said. "I'm sorry."

Chapter 12

During the following two days, Kyle phoned me several times, but I refused to answer his calls. I was not so much angry with Kyle as I was ashamed about what we had done. I believed that we were equally responsible for what had happened between us. Yet as guilty as I felt, I could not deny the pleasure I had experienced as Kyle's lips and body pressed against mine. In the days after our encounter, my recollection of each moment thrilled me, reigniting my desire. But at the same time, I badly regretted what had happened. I was consumed with the idea that Jed might find out, and I could hardly bear to imagine how he would respond to such knowledge. At times I felt overwhelmed with anxiety.

Jed also called me on several occasions during those two days. I tried to sound as upbeat and normal as possible, but I was always afraid that Jed might hear something in my tone to make him suspect something was wrong. During one such phone call, Jed expressed concern that he had not heard from Kyle and that that was unusual. He asked me if I had heard anything from him. As I considered the simple question, my heart sank and I felt sick to my stomach, realizing that I would have to lie to Jed. Clearly, I could not tell him that Kyle had in fact called me several times but that I had refused to speak to him. If I told him that, he would surely want an explanation for my behavior, and what could I say? With the pangs of guilt in my chest, I denied having heard from Kyle and made up some lame excuse that he must be working really hard. Jed seemed unconvinced, and I felt even worse knowing he was worried about his friend.

After a total of five days in the hospital, Jed was discharged with a clean bill of health. The doctors emphasized that he was really lucky that he had not suffered permanent brain damage. Rosa called me and told me that she was going to have a little celebration at her house that evening, and that I was invited, along with Kyle and the others who had been on the boat the day of the accident.

I was so anxious thinking about being around Jed, Kyle, and Hunter together, that I considered feigning illness to avoid attending the party. But I realized that it would not help me to stay away from them. If I was ever to see Jed again, or even Kyle, Brook, and Tyler, whom I now regarded as good friends, I knew would have to face the situation eventually.

Even as I grew increasingly stressed about the upcoming party, I took time readying myself in preparation for the event. I wanted to look as good as I could, in the hope that it would give me more confidence when I encountered the boys. I wore a low-rise denim miniskirt and lacy smock top that my grandmother had bought for me. I looked at myself in the mirror. My tanned legs looked long and lean, and the lacy shirt gave me a more feminine look than usual. I left my blond hair loose to fall about my shoulders. I contemplated my reflection. I looked older than I had just a few weeks earlier. I had lost weight, probably because I was hardly home long enough to eat a full meal. I thought I had grown, too, and I noticed that my face had changed. Gone was the babyish look of innocence that I remembered. I looked more mature and angular now, and I wore an expression of anxious concern that aged me further. I sighed heavily as I anticipated the challenges that lay ahead of me. "Okay," I said to the girl in the mirror as I pushed my hair behind my ears. "Let's do this thing." I took one last glance and then turned away from my reflection, scared yet determined to face whatever lay in store.

Though the sun was well into her descent, it was still light out as I rode my bike to Jed's house. The setting sun had painted the sky in a majestic array of warm colors, typical of a late summer evening. A fragrance of tropical flowers and seawater hung in the humid air that moistened my skin. The atmosphere about me was one of absolute tranquility, and yet I felt no peace of mind as I peddled my bike toward my destination.

When I arrived at Jed's house. I stopped outside the brightly painted garage door. So much had happened since I had first been astonished by the huge peace sign that seemed so out of place. Everything had been so simple back then. I smiled as I recalled my first meeting with Kyle and Jed. I shook my head and pondered the changes in my life since I had first encountered the boys. In retrospect, I had to admit that my life before then had been a little dull. But now everything seemed so complicated and messed up. I sighed as I considered all that had happened. "Well, at least it's not boring," I said to myself.

I entered the front door of Jed's house and looked around the room at all the people present, realizing I must have been the last to arrive. "There she is," said Rosa with a warm smile on her face. She stood with her arm around Jed as she conversed with Kyle's mother. She raised her hand and waved at me, appearing sincerely happy to see me.

Jed turned to face me, his mouth forming a wide grin as his eyes met mine. He walked over to me. "Hey, baby," he said as he embraced me, pulling my body close to his. I laid my head against his chest inhaling the familiar aroma of his young body. I closed my eyes, losing myself in the pleasure of the moment. I wanted to stay there in his arms forever, and yet I knew I would eventually have to face the other boys.

I opened my eyes, still resting my head against Jed's chest. Immediately Kyle's eyes caught mine as I realized he had been watching me. He sat in a chair just a few feet from where Jed and I stood, his eyes transfixed upon me. It felt as if his unfaltering gaze were cutting into me.

I looked at his face, trying to read his expression, but what he was feeling I couldn't tell. I thought he looked disappointed, maybe even hurt. Yet there was an essence of anger that seemed to emanate from him. I pulled my eyes from Kyle's and separated myself from Jed's embrace.

I began to sweat as I tried to clear my head and control my anxiety without being totally obvious. I looked up at Jed, making great effort to smile naturally. He appeared so happy and content as he smiled back at me, his innocent face so open and trusting. "Come on," he said as he led me by the hand to the kitchen. "Let's get you a drink and something to eat. He cocked his head. "Are you okay?" he asked with genuine concern. "You seem, I don't know, nervous or something."

"No, I'm fine. I'm just so happy you're home and everything," I said, trying to sound reassuring. In the kitchen, Jed poured two glasses of Coke. He handed one to me and raised his own in a toast.

"Here's to us," he said, as he looked into my eyes with affection. He took a sip and then set the glass on the counter. We were alone in the kitchen. Jed reached for me, wrapping his arm around my waist and pulling me close to him. "Do you have any idea how beautiful you are?"

he asked. I smiled, blushing with pleasure to be given such a compliment. "The whole time I was in the hospital, all I could think about was when I would finally be alone with you again." Jed's dark locks fell forward about his face as he looked down into my eyes. I could see myself reflected in the hypnotizing darkness of his irises as he gazed at me. His face was so close to mine that I could smell the sweetness of the soda on his breath. The rate of his breathing increased as I felt his body move against mine. He tightened his grip around my waist as he slowly lowered his lips toward my own.

Jed had kissed me before. But this time it was different. Gone were the soft, shy kisses with which I had become familiar. Now he pressed his lips firmly against mine, gently forcing them apart with his tongue so that the softness of our mouths entwined. It was as if all his emotion, all his happiness and sadness, his hopes and fears, and all his passion were being released in his kiss. As he poured himself into me, I felt an indescribable warmth and pleasure spreading through my body, filling me as if I were an empty vessel. I pressed myself closer to him, discovering that I too was able to let go of my fears, my shyness and lack of self-confidence expelled as I released myself into his kiss.

"At it again, I see. You like to get around, don't you, Rachel?" My heart skipped a beat as I recognized with horror the contemptuous voice of the person who had joined us in the kitchen. I hadn't heard Hunter's entrance, and I suspected he had snuck in after us for less than innocent reasons. I am sure my face turned crimson; it felt as if all the blood from my body rushed into my cheeks.

"What are you talking about?" asked Jed with a puzzled look on his face and a hint of annoyance in his tone.

"Ask your girlfriend," said Hunter, smirking as he grabbed a beer from the fridge. He unscrewed the cap from the bottle and flicked it across the room toward the garbage can. It hit the wall and landed with a ring on the tile floor. "Well…" He grinned maliciously as he stared at me. "See you later." He turned and left the room, and I thought I heard him snickering as he disappeared around the corner.

Jed looked down at me with a puzzled expression. "What's he talking about?" he asked as he released me. For a moment, I was speechless. I could hear my own pulse pounding in my brain, making it still harder for me to think. I swallowed hard, trying to think rationally as emotions flooded my mind. "Well?" said Jed impatiently.

I shrugged my shoulders and tried to look unconcerned. "How should I know?" I said nonchalantly. "You know how Hunter is, always trying to cause trouble. You shouldn't even bother with anything he says." Jed looked at me, staring into my eyes without even blinking. I felt as if he knew I was deceiving him. I looked back into his eyes, hoping I didn't look guilty. I had heard that people look a certain way when they're lying.

Suddenly he smiled as he reached back around my waist and pulled me close again. "You're right," he said. "The guy's an idiot."

I sighed with relief. At least for the moment, everything was okay, and it felt as if I could suddenly breathe fully again. I laid my head on Jed's chest, wishing we could just leave right then. Jed squeezed me tightly. "Mmm, I could stay just holding you all day, but I guess we'd better get back to the party." He let me go and started to walk toward the living room, and I reluctantly followed.

We joined the others and began to mingle with the small group. Just like at Jed's birthday party, Rosa had invited her hippie musician friends to play, and they asked Jed to join them in a jam session. Jed never looked more at home than when he was strumming some blues chords on his guitar, his feet and head moving to the rhythm. As his fingers moved up and down the instrument, his face contorted as he seemed to feel the whining notes of the melody in his soul. I loved to watch him play, because it was while he made music that Jed seemed to know exactly who he was and where he belonged. His hands moved with certainty across the strings, and he grinned contently at the other musicians as they melded together in harmony. Jed's eyes shone with an unequaled confidence as I watched him mesmerize his audience.

I was relieved that Jed had decided to jam right then because, by making it obvious that I was listening to him to play, I could avoid further socializing. Sometimes, I would steal a glance at Kyle, and whenever I did he appeared to be watching me. Jed and the others were really getting into the session, and I didn't think they were going to stop anytime soon. Feeling the constant gaze of Kyle upon my back was beginning to make me uncomfortable, so I headed to the kitchen to refill my drink.

"Rachel, can I talk to you for a second?" said the familiar voice behind me. I turned to see Kyle standing close to me. His expression was serious as his green eyes studied my face.

"Sure," I said. I could feel my stress level increasing by the second, as I was bombarded by the competing emotions of guilt, fear, and desire.

"Why didn't you answer any of my calls?" asked Kyle. He sounded genuinely hurt and confused, and I found myself feeling almost sorry for him.

"You know why," I said. "How could I talk to you?"

"No, I don't know why. Look, I know this is complicated, and I don't want Jed or anyone to get hurt, but I thought you felt something the other night. You sure acted like you did anyway." Now his tone was accusatory.

"Well, yeah, I did feel something, but…" I was lost for words.

"But what?" asked Kyle.

"Look, I really care about Jed, and what you and I did the other night wasn't right, especially since Jed was in hospital at the time."

"So what you're saying to me, then, is that it meant nothing to you and that you really don't care about me at all? I guess you were just being a tease, is that it?" The volume of Kyle's voice had increased, and his tone was caustic. I started to become worried that someone would hear us.

"Can you keep your voice down?" I said. "And that's not fair. You're the one who came on to me. Anyway, you yourself said you're too old for me."

"But we talked about that. Remember how I said I thought you were more mature, and my age didn't seem to bother you the other night. Plus, you know full well that you've been coming on to me ever since we met. It's obvious to everyone, so don't even try to deny it."

I felt the shame rise within me. Had it been that obvious? Clearly it had. I suddenly felt like a naive and stupid child. Maybe this whole mess was all my fault, and now everyone was going to blame me. To my horror, I felt my eyes filling with tears. "You don't have to be so mean," I whispered. "I'm sorry."

"Yeah, sure," said Kyle as he turned and walked away from me. I stood alone in the kitchen, as tears streamed down my face. In the distance, I heard Jed playing the now familiar sounds of the Grateful Dead. I sniffed and tried to regain my composure as I wiped my face with both hands.

It occurred to me that there were only a few weeks of summer left and that I would soon be heading back to England, Kyle would be leaving for his army training camp, and Jed would be left alone. Without Kyle, I doubted he would see much of the others. I wondered what lay ahead for each of us.

I stepped into the little bathroom and looked at myself in the mirror. I was a mess. My eyes were red from crying, and I felt emotionally exhausted. In the other room, I heard Jed's voice singing another tune I now recognized, "No Woman No Cry" by Bob Marley. I splashed cold water on my face and breathed deeply. "Okay then," I said to my reflection, "enough crying." And as I dried my face, the beautiful and melancholy words of the song seemed to sooth me.

I studied my face in the mirror. I was still so young, but I was changing in so many ways. Yes, I had made some mistakes this summer, but I was learning quickly from those mistakes. During the past few weeks, I had learned more about myself and about life and love than I had in all my previous years. Ready or not, I was starting to grow up. I only hoped that I would find enough strength to courageously face whatever challenges lay ahead.

Chapter 13

For the next few days, Jed and I were practically inseparable. I don't know if Kyle avoided us on purpose or if he just had to work a lot, but we saw very little of him. When we did see him, he barely made eye contact with me. He would say hello, but otherwise all his attention was given to Jed. Each encounter was short, as Kyle made excuses that he was in a hurry to go somewhere or other, and though in truth I was equally engaged in trying to avoid him, I was both hurt and annoyed by his behavior.

Still, I was generally very happy. I felt closer to Jed than I ever had before. I continued to worry about the time I kissed Kyle, and many times I considered confessing to Jed. But I knew how much pain it would cause him. I was afraid, too, that Kyle would be even angrier with me than he already was, and I didn't want Tyler and Brook to find out what I had done. So I stuffed my guilt and anxiety into a deep place within myself, where it could be ignored except for when I saw Kyle or Hunter. But when I lay alone in bed at night, the feelings would reemerge and torment me.

Though we spent most of our waking hours together, I always felt as if Jed and I never had enough time, especially as each day that came and went was a day closer to summer's end. The now familiar trails and beaches of Dunedin had become our own private paradise. We would wander aimlessly through the lush landscape, and many times we'd be so deeply engaged in conversation as to be oblivious to the world around us.

Initially, after Jed was released from the hospital, I had been reluctant to discuss the accident with him. But I was very curious about how he felt about the whole ordeal, and anyway, I sometimes felt as if maybe he wanted to talk about it. So on one afternoon as we strolled slowly down a deserted trail on Honeymoon Island, I summoned the courage to broach the subject. "Do you ever think about the accident?" I asked.

"Yeah, more than I want to," he responded.

"Well, what do you think about it?"

"I don't know, a lot of things," he said, shrugging. "It's all kind of foggy because there's a lot I don't remember. But then there are some things that are very vivid, you know?"

"Do you remember falling off the boat?" I asked.

"No." Jed shook his head. "No, all I remember is how Kyle was driving the boat really fast after he freaked out about that dumb joint."

"Do you feel like it was Kyle's fault, then?" I asked. I recalled Kyle's own confession of guilt, and the anguish he had expressed to me.

"No, not really. I mean, I do think he overreacted about the pot. And I know he was already pissed off that day and that was just an excuse to lay his own crap on me. But I'm sure he didn't think anyone was going to get hurt. Kyle's a good guy."

"I think he blames himself," I said.

"Yeah, I know. He's told me. But I keep telling him not to worry about it."

We walked for a while without speaking, as images from that day played in my consciousness like a slide show. Finally I spoke again. "What else do you remember from that day?"

"Nothing more from *that* day," he said. "But I remember stuff from when I was..." He hesitated as if unsure how to explain himself. "I guess from when I was unconscious." I looked at Jed and noticed he had a very distant look on his face as if his thoughts were far from the trail and the two of us. I waited for him to continue, because somehow it seemed inappropriate to disturb him at that moment.

"I remember feeling very peaceful," he said quietly as his eyes peered in my direction, and yet seemed to look right through me. "Everything was really bright and warm, and I knew I was safe, wherever I was. And then..." He smiled at me as he stopped walking and took both of my hands in his. "This is going to sound kind of weird, but I do really want to tell you."

"Okay, then," I said. I felt tense with curiosity and nervous anticipation.

"Well, I was there in that bright place," he said, shaking his head, "and I wasn't scared because it seemed like I knew where I was somehow. And then there was a man walking toward me." Jed smiled and looked into my eyes. "When he got close to me, I saw that he was my dad. He looked young, just like I had seen him in pictures before he died. He was really young, like Kyle, you know." He paused, as if he was remembering the image of his father.

I was captivated by the story. "Did he speak to you?" Jed nodded his head slowly. "Yeah, he did. I remember his words exactly. He smiled at me and he just said, 'Hi, son.'"

"Did you say anything back to him?" I asked.

"I just said hi back to him." Jed smiled and shrugged. "And then he said something else to me. He said 'It's not your time, son, but I'll be waiting for you. I'll see you then.' And then he just faded away."

"Was that all?" I asked.

"That was all with my dad. But then later I saw my mother and my grandmother. They were together. My mother, she looked beautiful. She looked young and healthy, and she was happy. She looked happier than I have ever seen her."

As Jed talked of his mother, his eyes softened with loving tenderness, and I was so moved by his expression that I had to look away from him. "You loved her a lot, didn't you?" I said quietly, forcing myself to look up at his young face.

"Of course, she was my mother. She was the most important person in my life when I was a kid, and I was still a kid when I lost her. I still miss her every day."

Jed inhaled deeply, momentarily holding his breath. He turned from me, and I knew he was hiding the emotion in his dark eyes from me, those dark eyes that never cried.

"It's okay," I said, as I stepped forward and placed my hand on his shoulder.

"I know," he answered, his voice cracking. "I'm fine, just give me one second." A few moments passed and then Jed turned to face me again. He smiled sadly. "I'm sorry," he said.

"Don't be," I told him.

"Anyway, my mother didn't speak to me. She just blew me a kiss the way she used to when she was alive." I smiled as I imagined this young, fair woman with flowing hair and dress, blowing her kisses at her bronze-colored son. I thought she might have looked like an angel.

"And your grandma, did *she* talk to you?"

Jed chuckled. "She said I should get my behind back where I belonged. She always knew how to get her point across."

The story was fascinating and somehow beautiful. "That's so amazing," I said. "It's like you were between two worlds or something."

"Yeah, well, that's not the end of it, though," he said, shaking his head. I was happy to hear this; I wanted to hear more.

"Later, when everyone else had faded away, you were there. You were there waiting for me."

My heart skipped a beat. It was thrilling to learn that I too had been present in Jed's dreams as he lay in his unconscious state. It was incredible. I smiled at him. "Really? That's so cool," I said.

"For real. You were there."

"Well, what did I do? What did I say to you?" I asked eagerly.

Jed smiled, and his eyes seemed to sparkle. "You said you were waiting for me." He took my hands again and held them firmly in his. "You said I should hurry back because you missed me and that there was still so much we hadn't done together. You told me I couldn't go yet." Jed paused, and I noticed my heart was beating rapidly. "Rachel, I'm alive because of you," he said quietly as he gazed into my eyes with absolute seriousness. "I really believe that. I'm here because I came back to be with you."

I sighed, overwhelmed by all I had just heard. "I'm so pleased that you did come back, Jed," I whispered as he embraced me. "I don't know what I would have done if I'd lost you."

We remained still and silent in each other's arms for some time, contemplating all that had happened. Eventually Jed released me. "Come on," he said, leading me down the trail by the hand." Let's go to our beach and eat. I'm starving."

"You're always starving," I teased as I lifted up his shirt and poked his ribs. "I don't get how you stay so skinny." He pulled me close to him and put his arm around my shoulder as we strolled slowly to the secluded little beach that had become *our* beach.

We laid out a blanket on the hot sand in an area that was shaded by palm trees and cypress trees. We had brought some snacks and cold drinks, and I felt completely relaxed as I made myself comfortable, gulping down an ice-cold soda and enjoying the feel of the liquid against my hot, dry throat.

I remembered the first time we had been on that beach alone together. That was the time Jed had told me about how he had taken his grandma's gun with the intention of shooting himself. I shuddered as I recalled the conversation.

"What are you thinking about?" asked Jed curiously. Apparently he had noticed my pained expression. I hesitated. I wasn't sure if I should mention the incident with the gun to him. "Rachel, you can talk to me about anything," he insisted, as if reading my mind.

"I was just thinking about when you brought Rosa's gun out here and, you know, what you were planning to do with it."

Jed remained quiet, as if he was thinking deeply. "You know," he finally said, "at that time, I would go to bed at night, and I would pray for sleep to come and take me away so I didn't have to wake up again. I felt like there was nothing left for me in life. But when I got out here with the gun, something made me stop." Jed sat up and crossed his legs crossed in front of him as he looked out to sea. In one hand, he held a long piece of grass on which he sucked. He shook his head. "It wasn't because I was afraid that I didn't do it," he continued. "But like I told you before, I remembered how much my grandparents had suffered when my mom died. And I thought about what it must have done to Rosa when my dad died. I didn't want to be responsible for causing anyone that much pain. And so I prayed." Jed turned to me and his deep dark eyes sparkled as a child's might when they have seen something magical. "I was never a religious kind of person, and I have hardly ever been to church, but I felt like I had no one else to turn to. And so I prayed to God that something would happen in my life to give me a reason to live." Jed smiled as he looked at me. "I guess someone was listening, because it wasn't long afterward that I met you."

I smiled. "I don't know what to say," I said quietly.

140

"There's nothing to say. It is what it is. It was destiny."

Chapter 14

Before the accident, Jed and I had talked openly with each other and without inhibitions. But physically, Jed had always been a little reserved and even shy in his expression of affection toward me. Ever since his release from the hospital, though, Jed's passion for life, and for me, was transparent. Whenever we were together, he would hold my hand or wrap an arm around me to hold me close to him. When we kissed, we allowed all of our emotion and desire to be expressed through the intimate dance of our mouths. We would kiss for what seemed like hours as Jed's fingers gently caressed the skin of my arms and face.

With the intensity of our relationship growing every day, I often found myself imagining just how intimate Jed and I would be willing to be before summer's end. In my heart and body, I felt capable and willing to go anywhere and do everything with Jed, but in my mind I wasn't nearly so sure. What I was sure of, however, was that the time would come when Jed and I would have to face that very decision, and I only hoped that I would be strong enough to make the right choice, whatever the right choice turned out to be.

The afternoon was particularly warm that day, as Jed and I sat alone in his room just talking and listening to music. The moment began with a simple kiss, much like the many other times that Jed had kissed me. At first he kissed me tenderly, and then his kissing became more pressured and exploring. I felt his body pushing against me, as he gently lowered me backward onto his bed. After I was fully reclined, we kissed for what seemed like a long time, as I seemed to sink into the bed under Jed's weight upon me. I felt as if I could have just kept on kissing him forever, but at some point he separated his mouth from mine and sat up, looking into my eyes all the while. He looked at me more intensely than ever before, and I almost felt a little scared. I felt my body beginning to tremble.

He pulled his T-shirt over his head and dropped it to the floor, revealing his skinny torso the color of caramel. He stroked the side of my face with his fingers without saying a word. I had the sense he was not able to express what he was feeling with words at that moment. He leaned forward slowly, lowering all of his weight upon me again as he began to kiss me tenderly once more. I smelled his familiar scent as the heat generated by the close proximity of our bodies caused him to begin to sweat. I felt his hands touching the skin of my waist, and then his hand moved delicately beneath my shirt until I felt him slowly exploring the curves of my chest. Again, I felt as if I was sinking into the bed, delighted by the touch of Jed's mouth, his hands, and his body.

But as I lay there, consumed by his presence, I felt a sudden sense of shame disrupt the blissful feeling I was experiencing. It was just a short while ago, I thought, that Kyle had been touching me in just the same way. The summer, it seemed suddenly, was passing by so quickly. Everything seemed to be moving so fast, and soon the summer would end. I suddenly felt anxious, and as if I was losing control.

Though Jed continued to kiss me with loving tenderness, internally I could feel myself becoming increasingly tense. I felt as if my mind and body were at odds with one another, as I grappled with conflicting emotions of anxiety, insecurity, and desire.

I opened my eyes when I felt Jed's mouth leaving my own. I watched silently as he propped himself up on one elbow, allowing his other hand to remain under my shirt. He looked at me thoughtfully and with affection in his dark eyes, and yet I could see concern in his face. "Is everything okay?" he asked. "You suddenly seemed kind of tense or something."

I smiled at him. His soft gaze and voice were so soothing. "I'm fine," I told him. "I'm just nervous." He stroked my hair and leaned forward to kiss me gently. "You're so sexy," he said. But as he spoke the words, I perceived some apprehension in his expression. "Rachel," he said nervously, "I've been thinking about how I feel about you. I want to be closer to you. I want to touch your whole body and see your whole body." He seemed almost afraid to look at me, and yet there was a longing in his eyes. "Do you want to get undressed with me?"

Although I had imagined this moment many times in my dreams, this had not been the question I had anticipated, and I found myself suddenly unsure of how to respond. I hesitated as I tried to consider the implications of the proposition, but I was so intoxicated with emotion and desire it was difficult to think clearly. "I…I don't know," I finally said in a voice that was more timid than I had intended.

I was not so naive as to not understand what Jed was suggesting to me, and I was excited by his desire to begin a sexual relationship with me. Without a doubt, there was a part of me that yearned for such intimacy. In so many ways, I wanted to feel closer to Jed, and my feelings of desire were as strong as anything I had ever experienced. Yet I was genuinely frightened. I had known girls in England who had had sex at my age, and I had considered them stupid and irresponsible. I had always thought of myself as too smart to do anything that could instantly change my life so drastically.

But there were other reasons for my hesitation. In less than two weeks, I would be returning to England. It was hard for me to imagine such a possibility, but what if I never saw Jed again? Already I hated to imagine how it was going to feel when I had to leave him. How would it be to have to leave him if we were involved in an intimate relationship? And if I was honest with myself, as much as I wanted Jed, I didn't really feel ready to take that step yet.

"What are you thinking?" asked Jed as he pulled his hand from beneath my shirt and began to stroke my hair.

I raised my hand to touch his arm as he positioned himself above me. "There is part of me that really wants to," I said, feeling heat in my cheeks and weakness in my body. "I mean not just to take off my clothes, but everything. Part of me wants to do everything with you. But I'm too scared."

"You don't have to be scared. I swear. I won't hurt you or let anything bad happen to you." He smiled tenderly at me. "I know what can happen—it happened to my parents, remember? But I have protection. I already have condoms, and we'll be really careful."

"It's not just that," I said, feeling suddenly childish and even ashamed of my reluctance. "I'm just not sure I'm ready." I looked away from him.

"Rachel," he said with some frustration in his voice, "I need you so much, and I swear I'll be careful." He paused momentarily. "And I know it'll make us closer." He looked into my face as he studied my eyes. "Do you love me?"

"I think so," I whispered.

"I think I love you, too," he whispered in response. He smiled at me. "And I want to make love to you."

"I do, too," I said, "but I'm not ready."

146

"But when will you be ready? You're leaving soon. I want to feel you before you go."

"That's the problem," I said. "Soon I'll have to go. What if I never even see you again?"

"Of course we'll see each other again. I'll make sure of it." He paused for a moment and just looked at me. "I can't believe this," he said as he sat up. He sounded hurt and even angry. "I thought we had something special." He turned away from me, his dark eyes colder now, and yet fully expressing his disappointment.

"We do," I said, "but this just doesn't feel right. Not now." My voice cracked as all my emotions began to overwhelm me and a flood of tears began to run down my cheeks. I felt that my tears were more the result of shock and indignant anger than sadness. I could hardly believe that Jed would treat me that way, and I was both heartbroken and furious.

But when Jed saw that I had started to cry, his face contorted and his lips began to tremble. "Oh God," he said in a tone of extreme concern as he wiped away my tears. "I'm so sorry. I can't believe I acted like that. I would never want to make you do something you didn't want to. I never want to hurt you. I'm such an asshole. Please, don't cry." Jed shook his head in dismay as he clenched his fists. "I'm so sorry," he said again, his eyes pleading. "It doesn't matter, I swear. I had just thought that you would want to, but really, it's not important. Just please don't cry."

For a moment, I was silent except for the irregular sniffing that my sobbing had induced. I took a deep breath as I struggled to regain my composure. The disappointment and hurt that I felt was still knotting my stomach. But I believed Jed with all my heart. I knew he was being truthful when he said he was sorry. "It's okay," I finally managed to say. My vision was still blurred with tears as I hastily wiped my face dry. I just wanted the moment to pass. I didn't want the tension between us to escalate any further. "I know," I sniffed. "I know you would never hurt me."

—

The summer's end drew ever nearer. In little more than a week, Kyle would be leaving for the army, and the following day I was to leave for England. The knowledge that we were soon to be separated by an ocean affected Jed and me like a bad headache. The more we thought about it, the more painful it became. And so we did our best to ignore this reality and to enjoy the little time we had left.

It was always hardest at night when I laid alone in my room. I would try to concentrate on all the good times Jed and I had shared together, reminding myself that just a few hours remained before I would see him again. But each night eventually led me back to the image of Jed and me exchanging our last good-bye, and my lonely trip back to England.

When I left England, I had left a place where I had felt like I spent almost all of my time alone. With my parents always at work, the many hours I was left alone writing my poetry and reading sometimes seemed endless, and rarely did I have the pleasure of enjoying the companionship of others. I imagined myself back in London as the shy and lonely child I was when I left. It was sickeningly humiliating to recall the self-conscious and awkward girl I was before I arrived in Dunedin this time. I remembered how I would watch the other girls who attended my school or who lived in my neighborhood, and how I would envy the ease with which they laughed together as they had fun, not only among themselves, but also with boys.

But this summer had been different for me. From the first time I had met the boys on the little pier downtown, something had changed within me. I had felt suddenly bolder than I ever had before. It was as if I had suddenly been stripped of a protective coating as I stepped out into a world where I could allow myself to feel, even if that left me vulnerable. At that moment, I was no longer a child, but a teenage girl on her journey toward womanhood. It was a little scary, as I recognized that I was experiencing new and unfamiliar terrain. But I was so excited about the summer and all it could bring that even then I knew I wanted more.

I recalled all the hot and humid days that had come and gone since that first encounter, and it amazed me how much I had changed. I had grown in confidence and self-assuredness. I had abandoned the awkward, bookish child with whom I had become so familiar, and from her shell had emerged a vibrant young woman, alive with sexuality and adventure. But more importantly, I had found a new sense of courage, a quality that had enabled me to express and stand up for myself.

And yet soon I was to return to the home I had left just weeks before. Would I lose her? Would I lose the person I had become, the girl who had learned to love and live for the first time in her life? Would the young woman who had had the courage to speak up for what she believed to be right just disappear? Would I then shrink back into the protective wrap that had encased me before I had arrived?

Or could I continue to be who I was now? Was this confident, attractive girl, who had a boy to love, and friends, and strength—was she really me? Would I be able to hold onto her, or would she stay behind with Jed and the others?

No, that couldn't be possible, for I had changed. The experiences of the summer were part of who I had become, and the memories would be with me always. How I would adapt to life back in England only time would tell. But I had no doubt that life would be different for me now.

As there was so little time left before we parted, Jed and I made a point of trying to spend every possible moment together. I became so comfortable in his house that sometimes I would just stay there alone and wait for him if he had to go somewhere without me for a while.

One afternoon, just days before I was to leave, I sat alone on Jed's bed waiting for him to return from his guitar lesson. I had grown accustomed to the old rock music he enjoyed, and I was listening to a CD by Carlos Santana, who had become one of my favorite artists. I loved the way the notes of his guitar seemed to sing and dance on the Latin rhythms of the drums as they filled the small room.

The music was loud, which is probably why I did not hear Kyle and Hunter entering the house. As I had not been expecting them, I jumped in fright when Jed's bedroom door suddenly flew open and the boys practically fell in.

Both boys appeared a little different from their usual selves, especially Hunter, whose blue eyes were bloodshot and half-closed. "Hey," said Kyle, looking surprised to see me. "What are you doing here?" His speech was a little slurred, and his body appeared to weave a little from side to side.

Hunter took a couple of unsteady steps backward and propped himself against a wall. He pulled a bottle from the deep pocket of his shorts and unscrewed the cap. He took a swig of the straw-colored liquid in the bottle and swallowed hard. Afterward he exhaled loudly. "Do you want some?" he asked me in muffled words. He extended the bottle toward me.

"What is it?" I asked, feeling rather unnerved and yet somewhat intrigued by the two drunken teenagers who had just interrupted me.

"Tequila," explained Kyle. "It's pretty strong, maybe you shouldn't have any."

"Sure, I'll try some," I said without hesitating. Kyle's green eyes locked with mine as we exchanged glances that seemed to challenge each other.

"That a girl," said Hunter, winking as he handed me the bottle. "Suck some down."

I raised the bottle and took a large defiant gulp of the liquid. The taste, odor, and sensation of the liquor took my breath away as I swallowed. I began gasping for air. I had not expected it to taste so toxic, and I felt it burning as it slipped down the middle of my chest and into my stomach.

"I warned you," said Kyle, appearing a little concerned. "Are you okay?"

"Yeah," I coughed between gasps as I tried to hide my embarrassment. "I guess I'm not used to drinking stuff that strong."

"What kind of stuff are you used to drinking, then?" slurred Hunter as I handed the bottle back to him.

The truth was that I had hardly drunk alcohol at all except for the one time I'd had beer with Kyle. I did remember being given a little champagne at my aunt's wedding, though. "Mostly just beer and champagne," I told him, trying to sound matter-of-fact about it.

"Yeah, you probably have had champagne. I bet it was the expensive shit, too," said Kyle. He indicated to Hunter to pass him the tequila. He took the bottle and wiped off the top with the bottom of his T-shirt. "This is about as close to champagne as I've ever come, frigging cheap tequila. Cheers, princess!" He raised the bottle to me. Then he took a long swig. "You want some more?" he asked, handing me the booze.

"What are you two doing here anyway?" I asked, ignoring Kyle's obvious badgering about my parents' wealth. I raised the bottle to my lips, this time more prepared for the experience of what I was sure was comparable to drinking cleaning fluid.

"Hunter wanted to get a copy of Jed's Nirvana CD," explained Kyle. "Where is Jed anyway?"

"Oh, he's at his guitar lesson," I said. Already my head was beginning to feel a little heavy and I felt a giddiness coming over me. "You're right," I said, smiling and looking at Kyle, "this tequila is really strong."

"Have some more," said Hunter. He grinned mischievously. "It's good for you."

"Oh really?" I said sarcastically.

"You'll make her puke, man," said Kyle, looking at Hunter with annoyance.

"She's a big girl. You can handle it, can't you, babe?" Hunter slurred, as he watched me through half-closed, red eyes. "But," he continued, grinning in Kyle's direction, "I guess you know that about her better than anyone, eh, Kyle?"

"What?" grunted Kyle.

"You know what I mean."

"Whatever," said Kyle with some annoyance.

My head was feeling heavier, but the pleasant giddiness of early intoxication left me feeling loose and relaxed. I raised the bottle to my lips once more. The harsh beverage, I noticed, had become somewhat more palatable.

"So did you ever finish the job?" Hunter asked, looking in Kyle's direction.

"What are you talking about?" responded Kyle, his eyes heavy with drunken sleepiness.

"You know what I'm talking about. Did you ever finish doing her?" He jerked his head in my direction.

"No, man." Kyle shook his head as he looked at me. His words had become more slurred than when he had first arrived. "I tried, but she wouldn't let me. She wouldn't even talk to me, would you, Rachel?"

I felt suddenly guilty and ashamed, as if I had done something terribly wrong. My face felt hot with embarrassment, or perhaps it was the liquor that ran through my blood. "Well," I said defensively, "Jed was in the hospital. It didn't seem fair."

"That didn't seem to bother you while we were making out," said Kyle as he stretched out his hand and indicated for me to pass him the bottle.

"Yeah," said Hunter. "What's up with that, Rachel? Because you sure seemed to be having a good time when I busted in on you guys." His face expressed contempt. "Are you telling us you didn't like it and that you're just another tease?"

"No," I argued. "I mean, I wasn't being a tease. It just happened."

"Well, were you having a good time with me or what, because it sure seemed like it to me." Kyle peered at me, his eyelids heavy on his green, bloodshot eyes.

I leaned my head back against the wall behind me as the alcohol ran through my veins, warming my body. I was beginning to feel a bit queasy. I closed my eyes and noticed I had a sense of being in a small boat that was swaying from side to side. I thought back to the evening that Kyle had kissed me, and the memory brought with it the familiar and pleasant excitement I had experienced that night, before Hunter interrupted us. "I liked it," I admitted.

As I spoke, the bedroom door opened and Jed entered with enthusiasm. "Hey," he said, smiling enthusiastically. He stopped suddenly, as his expression changed to one of confusion. He looked at me. "What's wrong, Rachel?" he asked. He sounded concerned.

"Tequila," interrupted Hunter. Jed turned abruptly to see who had spoken. "She's been drinking tequila," Hunter explained, with a drunken smile.

"What's going on? What are you doing in here?" asked Jed as he turned to see Kyle slouching on the floor with the almost empty bottle of booze in his hand.

"We just came to borrow a CD, that's all. But we ended up talking to your girlfriend here, didn't we, Rachel?" Kyle looked at me and his drunken eyes expressed contempt.

"And getting her drunk," snapped Jed, obviously upset. "Whose idea was that?"

153

"She wanted to partake," said Hunter. "It was her choice. She's no innocent little girl, you know. Truth is, buddy, she's probably more woman than you can handle."

"What are you talking about?" asked Jed sounding even more irritated and confused.

"Ask Kyle, dude," said Hunter, smirking. "Or better yet, ask your girlfriend. She knows what I'm talking about, don't you, Rachel?"

"What's going on here, Rachel?" Jed looked worried, almost scared.

"Nothing," I lied. My head was spinning, and I now felt very nauseated. "I just had a couple of sips of that stuff and we were just talking." I felt my cheeks aflame with shame and guilt as the lie escaped clumsily from my lips.

"Oh, come on, honey," interrupted Hunter. "Don't be shy, tell the kid the truth."

"Shut up, Hunter, man," said Kyle, as he finished the last of the tequila.

"Why?" said Hunter, with sarcasm in his voice. "You don't think he has a right to know?"

"A right to know what?" asked Jed, anxiety apparent on his young face.

"Just forget about it," instructed Kyle authoritatively. But Jed just appeared to become more anxious as I heard a growing urgency in his tone.

"Rachel, are you going to tell me what everyone is talking about or not?"

I stared back into those dark eyes and was suddenly aware that I had developed double vision. I wondered which of Jed's two faces I should look at.

"Well?" he pressed. But I could not find the words. I looked away, dizzy, ashamed, and just praying I that I wouldn't throw up in front of everyone.

Jed turned to Hunter. "Just tell me," he demanded.

"It's no big deal," said Hunter, smiling maliciously. "It's just that while you were near dead in the hospital, these two got freaky together. I walked in on them myself."

Jed swung his body around to face me, his face contorted with emotion. "Is that true?" He looked deeply into my eyes as I tried to focus on his two faces.

"It's not how he made it sound," I whispered. "It was nothing, just a kiss, that's all." I could hear myself slurring my words as I spoke, and I was surprised by how drunk I really was.

"I think it was more than that, babe," said Hunter. "And weren't you just telling us how much you liked it right before he walked in here?"

"Shut the hell up," yelled Kyle, stumbling to his feet.

"What's your problem?" Hunter swayed as he stood looking at Kyle. "It's time you finished what you started with her anyway. What are you, some kind of a pussy?"

"Hunter, man, don't be an asshole," Kyle said more quietly, as he leaned against the wall to support himself.

"Hell, man, if you're not going to do her, then I am. She's pretty much been begging for it for the whole summer." Hunter stumbled toward Jed. He leaned in toward him, resting his hand on Jed's shoulder, steadying himself as he moved his face close to his ear. Jed winced at the pungent odor of his breath. "Why don't you run along now, kid?" slurred Hunter. "Kyle and I have got some unfinished business to take care of in here."

Jed jerked his shoulder free of Hunter's grip. "Get the hell off me," he commanded. "Rachel, let's get out of here now, come on." Jed tried to move toward me, but Hunter pushed him back toward the door. "Get up, Rachel," yelled Jed with panic in his voice. I started to get up, frightened by the situation.

"Sit the hell down, Rachel, before I knock you down," growled Hunter. Frightened by his aggression, I did exactly as he instructed. He continued to push Jed back toward the open door.

155

Though Kyle leaned against the wall, he could barely stand. He was so intoxicated that he stood with bent legs as he leaned forward and supported himself by resting his arms on the front of his thighs. He raised his head and attempted to focus on Hunter through half-closed eyes. "Come on, man. Leave him alone. Let's just get the CD and get out of here."

"I'm not hurting him," grunted Hunter in response. "He just needs to get gone for a while."

Jed now stood in the doorway. He looked frightened and bewildered. "I'm not leaving without Rachel," he said defiantly.

"You don't have a choice," said Hunter, laughing. "Now get lost." Hunter gave Jed a final hard push that knocked him off balance. He fell onto his behind, slamming his head hard on the wall behind him. Hunter slammed the door and locked it.

I was getting dizzier by the second, and I was sure I was going to vomit. I tried to grasp what was happening, but my mind was so foggy I just felt confused. I knew that Hunter meant trouble, but somehow I believed with Kyle there I was safe. I did not believe he would let anything bad happen to me. My eyelids felt heavy and I wanted to sleep. I was brought back to the reality of the moment by the sound of the door being rattled, and to my relief I knew Jed was trying to reenter the room. "I told you to piss off," yelled Hunter. "You better get out of here before I come out there and kick your ass, kid." Hunter approached the bed where I was sitting. I stared at the door, praying that Jed would not give up, but the rattling stopped and I heard Jed's footsteps running down the hall and away from me. My heart sank.

"So, Rachel," said Hunter. His massive body swayed above me, trapping me on the bed. "Tell us again how much you liked it. How much did you like Kyle's tongue down your throat? Because there's more of that to come." I looked at Hunter's face as he leered at me. I was so embarrassed. As dazed and confused as I was, it was beginning to dawn on me that I was truly in big trouble. Now I was

156

starting to get really scared. I tried to figure out what I could do to stop the situation from going any further.

"Just leave me alone, Hunter," I said, trying to sound firm and forceful.

"What?" he said, laughing at me. "You think you can tell *me* what to do now? I think I was the one asking *you* a question. I asked you to tell me how much you liked it when Kyle was feeling you up."

My face flushed red as I recalled how Hunter had walked in and seen Kyle with his hand under my shirt.

"Well," said Hunter, "you did say you liked it. So, did you or didn't you?"

"Well, yes, but—"

"But what?" Hunter interrupted. "You liked it, but you're a little tease." His sarcasm sliced into me like a sharp knife. He turned to Kyle. "So, are you going to finish her off, or what?"

Kyle looked at me. In his bloodshot eyes, I saw uncertainty and apprehension. "If she wants me to, I will," he finally said, almost sulkily.

"Of course she wants you to. You know yourself that she's been begging for it since she met you." Hunter looked at me as I sat silently on the bed. I was shaking now, though I still felt sure that Kyle would not hurt me. It was Hunter that I was afraid of. At least my fear was sobering. "Plus," continued Hunter, "you need to put her in her place. She needs to learn a lesson. She needs to know that she can't just lead guys on and then not put out. You need to set her straight. Or are you too much of a pussy to do that?"

"Shut up," said Kyle, obviously agitated by Hunter's comments. "You're crazy." Kyle looked at me, and I could see how nervous and uncomfortable he was. "Rachel, do you want me to..." He hesitated as his face reddened. He was obviously as embarrassed as I was. "You know what I mean—do you want to have sex with me?"

I shook my head, too afraid now to even speak. Hunter laughed. He narrowed his eyes as he stared at me. The expression on his face was cruel and controlled. "Don't worry about what she says, man. I'm telling you she wants it. Don't be such a frigging wimp. I thought I taught you to handle your women better than that."

"First of all, she's not my woman, she's just a kid," said Kyle, raising his voice. "And you really are crazy if you think I'm going to bang a chick who doesn't want me to." Hunter's face reddened and contorted with anger. "Whatever. You're a pussy," he said sarcastically. "But I'm going to give it to her. The little rich bitch has had it coming. I'm telling you, she's been coming on to us all summer. You know you want me to ride you, don't you?" He sat down on the bed beside me and put his hand on my knee.

"Please, Hunter," I whispered. My body trembled violently with fear as tears began to prick at my eyes.

He laughed. "You don't have to beg me," he said. "I'm already there." Suddenly he was on his knees on the bed. His big hands on my shoulders forced me backward as he collapsed his entire weight on me. He was so heavy I could hardly breathe.

"Come on, Hunter. Get off her. This isn't funny," yelled Kyle.

"I'm not trying to be funny," grunted Hunter. His breathing had become hard and heavy, and I smelled the reek of alcohol each time he exhaled. His hand was suddenly on my chest as he squeezed my breast so hard that for a moment I could not catch my breath. The pain was excruciating. I screamed, but he covered my mouth with his other hand, silencing me. He used his legs to force mine apart as he pressed his hardened body against my pelvic bone. I used all the strength I had to try to get out from under him, but it was no use. He was so heavy and so much stronger than me. I thought about trying to bite him, but I couldn't move my head. Out of the corner of my eye, I looked at Kyle, begging him with my eyes to do something to help me, as I continued to try to free myself from Hunter's

158

tremendous weight. But when I made eye contact with Kyle, he just looked helpless and turned away from me.

As panic mounted within me, I tried even harder to fight off Hunter, but he was so heavy that it was useless, and I could feel my body tiring from the effort. His hand left my bruised breast, and I felt him push it forcefully between my legs. He moved his other hand between us to the button of my pants.

Suddenly, there was a loud crash as the bedroom door flew open. Jed entered the room. He had a crazed look upon his face as tears streamed down his cheeks. He stared at Hunter on top of me, and then he raised both of his arms in front of him. In his hands was a gun, which he pointed directly at Hunter. "Get off her or I'll blow your brains out, I swear to God."

Jed's voice cracked, but his tone was bitter with hatred.

"You better watch where you wave that thing or someone's liable to get killed," said Hunter as he watched Jed's shaking hands warily.

"I'm not kidding, you asshole. I swear if you don't get off her, I'll pull the trigger and splatter you all over this room."

"Jed," said Kyle, his voice shaking with fear. "Put the gun down before you hurt somebody."

"You stay out of this, you worthless piece of shit. You weren't even going to try to help her. What kind of man are you? What kind of soldier do you think you're going to be when you can't even stand up for a friend?" said Jed angrily.

Kyle looked down at the floor as if defeated by Jed's words.

"Just put the gun down, Jed," he said sulkily. "I don't want you or anyone to get hurt."

Jed ignored Kyle as he kept his eyes fixed on Hunter. I lay petrified, almost too scared to breathe. It occurred to me that if Jed shot the gun, he might actually kill me. I tried to swallow, but my mouth was too dry.

"I'm going to count to three, and then I'm taking you out," said Jed with determination. As he tightened the grip of his hands

159

around the gun, his shaking stopped. He slightly adjusted his aim as he began to count slowly. "One...two..." Hunter laughed nervously as he began to lift the weight of his body off me. "It's not worth it," he said as he stood up. He walked slowly toward Jed and pointed his finger close to Jed's face. "You better watch out, little man, because you're going to be sorry you messed with me." Jed opened his mouth as if he was about to say something to Hunter, but Kyle beat him to it. "Get the hell out of here you fat-ass jerk," said Kyle, looking at Hunter with disdain. "And if you threaten him again, I'll kill you myself. Do you understand me?"

Hunter seemed shocked by Kyle's words. He looked at Kyle and laughed, the spite apparent in his expression. "I guess you're as pathetic as they are. You're all losers." He looked at both me and Jed before he walked out the door.

I lay on the bed, still shaking. I sensed that I was breathing very rapidly, and my heart felt as if it was going to explode. The tears streamed down my face, but I was still too scared to allow the sobs that jolted my chest to escape from my throat.

Jed walked over to the bed and sat down, taking my hand in one of his. I saw that the other hand, the one in which he still held the gun, had started to tremble again. "Are you okay?" he asked quietly and tenderly, with concern in his eyes. "Are you hurt?" I shook my head in response.

"I'll get her some water to drink," said Kyle, as he watched us from across the room.

"Don't bother," said Jed without looking at him. "Just leave."

"Listen, Jed," pleaded Kyle.

"No! I don't want to listen to you, and I have nothing to say to you. Just get the hell out."

Kyle slowly shook his head as he turned away and headed for the door. As I watched him go, I saw the sadness in his green eyes.

Chapter 15

After what happened with Hunter, Jed I talked about whether I should tell my grandparents or go to the police. But I was afraid, and in the end I chose to tell no one. For years afterward, there would be times when I regretted my decision. It occurred to me that the fear that kept me from holding Hunter accountable for his actions might ultimately have enabled him to hurt others. But more than that, I eventually came to realize that by not confronting Hunter myself, I was unable to let go of the pain he had caused me.

But at the time, all I could think about was forgetting the whole ordeal, and spending as much time as possible with Jed before I returned to London. I was afraid that if my parents found out what had happened, I might not be allowed to see Jed again or, even worse, that Jed might get in trouble for the gun and

161

for threatening to kill Hunter, and then he would never be able to see me.

Jed and I did talk about that day and everything that had led up to it, though. At first it was really hard for both of us. Jed was so mad. He hated Kyle almost as much as he hated Hunter. And he was also still really mad at me for kissing Kyle. Initially, he could barely look me in the eyes.

"I just don't understand how you could have done that to me," he would say, and the pain in his voice and on his face made my own heart ache with regret. I couldn't explain what had happened between Kyle and me to Jed. I didn't even understand it myself. And even though I felt so sorry for all the pain my actions had caused, when I thought about the time that Kyle and I had been together, I still couldn't help but feel a certain warm pleasure that only compounded my guilt. But of course, it was impossible for me to share these feelings with Jed.

At other times, when I thought about what had happened with Hunter, and what he might have done, I would cry, and Jed would hold me as he tried to comfort me. He tried to understand how I felt, but there was no way to convey the humiliation and terror I had felt that day.

And so those late summer days came and went, and as Jed and I grappled with all that had happened, for the first time in our relationship I think we both realized there were some things we could not share with each other. And yet, for all that we could not share, there was so much more that we did understand about each other now, without even trying to. Emotionally, our relationship had become truly intimate, and I had never felt as close to anyone before.

So these were to be the last days we would spend together. Before, I had imagined us spending the hours blissfully in love and content in all except for the reality of our impending separation. But life had had other intentions for us, and in many ways those days proved to be painful for Jed and me, both as individuals and in our relationship. And yet the series of events that had brought us to this place had united us in ways neither one of us could have imagined before. In my heart, I believed Jed had rescued me from a fate I did not care to imagine. Had it not been for him, I was sure that Hunter would not have stopped until he had hurt me, and I was eternally grateful to Jed for his bravery.

I did not doubt for one second that Jed would have pulled the trigger if Hunter had not released me when he did, and I was both frightened and impressed by the ruthlessness and raw courage that he revealed that day. I shuddered as I imagined how close we all came to being the players in some awful tragedy that surely would have delighted the local media. Yes, Jed had proven himself my hero.

Like Jed, initially I had felt a great deal of contempt and resentment toward Kyle. He had, after all, just stood there watching as that big animal had humiliated and assaulted me, all the while doing nothing to help me. I couldn't understand why he had not made more of an effort to stand up to Hunter. Perhaps it was because Kyle had always admired and looked up to him, or perhaps he was just too afraid. And yet when Hunter threatened to hurt Jed, Kyle had confronted him in no uncertain terms. Why couldn't he have done the same for me?

But the darkest thoughts with which I struggled in those hours and days after the attack involved dealing with my own feelings of guilt and responsibility. I knew that what Hunter had done was horrendous and unforgivable. But deep down I couldn't help wondering if the things he had said were true. I remembered with some horror all the times I had flirted with Kyle and how much I had wanted him. I remembered how easily I had succumbed to his kisses and how willing I was to accept his affections. How could I have been so stupid when I was alone with them, both of them drunk, as to tell them how much I had enjoyed the intimacy that Kyle and I had shared? Perhaps I had encouraged them. Perhaps it was my fault. But I knew that this could not be true. There were no excuses or reasonable explanations for what Hunter had done and for what Kyle had failed to do. And yet still I was tormented by my own sense of shame and guilt.

Of course I could not discuss these thoughts with Jed. First of all, I was afraid that Jed, too, might start to believe that I was somehow to blame for what had happened. And secondly, I didn't want to hurt him any more by rehashing the things that had happened between Kyle and me. And so I suppose that Jed and I suffered in silence, as we each battled our own demons. And yet I sensed that together we were already rewriting our young relationship, a relationship that too soon had developed a sordid history that would leave wounds that would take a long time to heal.

Three days before I was scheduled to leave, I got a call from Kyle. It was late, past ten at night, when he called, and seeing his name on my phone took me by surprise. I had not heard from him since the ordeal with Hunter, and of course I was very reluctant to speak with him. Yet there was a part of me that wanted to confront him and to tell him how he had failed me and failed to stand up for what was right. I wanted him to know how much he had hurt me.

"Rachel," he said, after I reluctantly answered the call. "I know you probably don't even want to hear my voice, but I really need to talk to you." He sounded sad, almost desperate, and I actually found myself feeling a little pleasure in his pain.

"Okay," I said, "I'm listening."

"I mean I want to talk to you face-to-face," he said with some urgency. "I don't feel right talking about this over the phone."

I felt the familiar tug of nervous anxiety as my heart rate quickened. First of all, I wasn't at all sure that I wanted to see Kyle yet or ever. And anyway, it was past ten, and I knew my grandparents would not agree to me going out at this hour. I could hear Kyle breathing through the phone as he waited for my response, but I couldn't think of the right words.

"Please, Rachel," he pleaded. "I really need to see you."

"I can't," I explained. "I'm not allowed out this late."

"Well, that's okay," he said without hesitation, "I can come over if it's all right with you. We can talk on your porch, if I can't come in." I could hear the desperation in his voice.

It was against my better judgment, but there was something about Kyle that was so persuasive even as he begged pathetically over the phone. It seemed almost impossible for me to resist him. "Okay," I sighed, already regretting my decision. "I'll meet you on the porch."

Outside, I settled myself on the porch swing and gently swayed back and forth. There was no breeze, and the night air was still quite thick and hot as the sound of crickets and bullfrogs filled the stillness of the night. An elderly gentleman wandered slowly by as he walked a small, white dog on a leash. He waved briefly at me, and I smiled back as he passed by. After a while, I heard the sound of a car turning onto the quiet street, and I saw headlights moving toward the house. As the familiar little truck slowed and then parked in front the house, I felt a nauseating fluttering in my abdomen as I anticipated seeing Kyle. The car door opened and I caught my breath.

As he walked toward me in his long, baggy shorts that hung below his knees and his dark T-shirt, he looked down at the ground, concern aging his young face. At the stairs to the porch, he stopped and looked up at me, briefly smiling, but his eyes looked sad.

"Hey," he said.

"Hey," I responded.

He walked up the stairs slowly and deliberately. "Mind if I sit down?" he asked indicating the swing with his eyes.

"All right," I answered, moving to one side to make room for him. He sat beside me and laid his hands in his lap, and for a while we just sat there swinging together in silence.

"So what did you want to talk to me about?" I finally asked, frustrated by the silence.

"I'm sorry," said Kyle. "This is hard for me." He spoke quietly and I noticed him wringing his hands. "Look, Rachel, first let me tell you how sorry I am about what happened with Hunter. I know how terrible that must have been for you." As he spoke, his eyes stayed focused on his hands and I knew he was avoiding looking at me.

"I doubt very much you could possibly understand how terrible it was," I said sarcastically and with indignation. I could feel the emotion rising in my throat.

Kyle's face flushed deep red, and he appeared momentarily flustered. "You're right," he said apologetically. "I didn't mean to suggest that I know how you felt, but…I'm sure it was terrible, and I feel…" He hesitated as if he was having a hard time explaining himself. "I'm just really sorry that it happened like that." He sounded emotionally exhausted.

"Well," I said, unsympathetically, "it was, like you said, terrible. I was totally humiliated and scared to death, and the whole thing has left me completely freaked out, and Jed, too. And one of the worst things about it is that you barely did anything to try to stop him. I don't understand what you were thinking. I thought we were friends. I thought you were better than that."

My throat ached as I struggled to hold back the tears that threatened to spill in a flood of emotion. I looked at Kyle and saw that he was bent forward with his elbows on his knees and his head in his hands.

The tension between us was intense, and I felt as if I wanted to hit Kyle, and scream at him, expressing and freeing all the pain within me. And yet he looked so pathetic, and even remorseful, that something deep in my gut made me restrain myself even though I felt as if acid were burning a hole through the front of my chest. I regretted my decision to meet him, but I knew that this moment had to come and that I would have had to face him eventually.

Kyle sighed loudly and sniffed as he wiped his face vigorously, trying to regain control. He turned and looked directly at me, and his sad green eyes were wet with tears. "Rachel," he said

166

through lips that trembled with emotion. He shook his head sadly. "I don't know why Hunter acted like that, and I don't know why I didn't intervene more. I have no excuse.' He paused, inhaling deeply and blew out his breath as if calming himself. "Look, Hunter was always a jerk to girls. He treated his girlfriends like crap. But I never, ever would have expected him to do something like that, I swear. I would never have hung out with him." He turned away from me and looked out into the darkness of the night. "I told you his dad was a really violent guy, especially to his mom. I'm not trying to make excuses for what Hunter did, but maybe he's got those problems because of the things he watched his dad do."

"Maybe," I said dryly. "But you're right, that doesn't give him an excuse to do what he did. And it doesn't change the fact that you did nothing to stop him."

"I know," said Kyle. His voice was remorseful and resigned. "I wish I could explain, but I can't. I've tried to understand what I was thinking at the time, but..." Kyle seemed unable to finish his sentence. Instead he just shook his head and shrugged his shoulders, a look of bewilderment on his face. "I guess Hunter always had some power over me, ever since we were young." Kyle looked at me with an expression of defeat upon his young face, but in his eyes I could see sincerity. "I suppose I was scared to stand up to him. I'm sorry I let you down, Rachel." Kyle turned from me and laid his head back against the swing, folding his arms across his chest. "Jed's right," he whispered. "I am worthless. I was worthless to you, to Jed, to my parents, and I'll probably be worthless as a soldier, too.'

Much to my dismay, I realized I was beginning to feel just a little sorry for Kyle, but not enough to let it go. I needed to confront him further; I wanted more from him. Even though he claimed to have accepted responsibility for his failure to help me, I needed to know when, if ever, he would have tried to do something. "Kyle, what if Jed hadn't come in, and Hunter had really been able to go through with—" I hesitated, trying to decide how to phrase my question. I felt a pang in my heart, but a wave of angry determination seemed to empower me, and I knew the words to use. I began to speak again. "What if Hunter really intended to rape me? Would you just have stood there watching and done nothing?"

"I want to say no. I really do. I want to say I would have stopped him and helped you, that I would have killed him if I had to. But if you want me to be honest…" He shook his head. "All I can say is I don't know. I just don't know."

He turned his head to look at me, and we stared at each other for a few moments. I felt as if we were both naked. Not in a sexual way, but as if we were fully and honestly exposing ourselves in our most vulnerable form. The truth lay between us, and we would have to deal with it as best we could. I nodded my head and turned away from him, sighing deeply, and as I released the breath, I felt the weight that had been suffocating me lighten just a little.

"Okay," I finally said. "I think I'm going to be okay." I turned to look at Kyle's worn young face. "But you know what, Kyle? You need to be better. You need to be stronger. You need to be more of a man, and you need to have some honor. You've got to be more like the person you pretended to be when I first met you, the person I admired so much." I felt my own face soften just a little as I observed the tension in his. It surprised me how calming it felt to let go of some of my anger.

"You're right," he said. "You're totally right. I just hope that I can be a better person." For some time, we just sat in silence, slowly swinging back and forth. I looked up at the multitude of stars that dotted the blackness of the night sky, and I considered that very soon I would be back in London where it's hard to see the stars because of light pollution. My thoughts wandered, and I imagined once again how my life in London would be now that this summer had changed everything.

I was abruptly reminded of the reality of the moment by the sound of Kyle's voice. "There's something else I need to talk to you about," said Kyle quietly.

I turned to him. My pain and anger had lessened significantly, and I felt surprisingly peaceful. "What?" I said.

Kyle's eyes still reflected tremendous sadness, though, and I could see he was still struggling. "It's Jed," he said, looking down at the ground, shame and guilt upon his face. "He won't even talk to me."

"Well, he's angry right now," I explained gently. "Can you blame him?"

"I know, and he has every right to be pissed with me, of course. But tomorrow night I leave for North Carolina, and after basic training I don't know how long I'll get home for, or if I'll even get to come home before I get deployed somewhere, you know, what with the war and all. I don't want to go with this…this mess between us."

"You really care about him, don't you?" I said.

"It's hard to believe after some of the ways I've screwed up, but yeah. It's like I told you, I was never really that close to anyone, before. But with Jed, I felt like maybe I could make a difference. Do you understand what I'm trying to say?"

"Yeah, I think so." From the first day I'd met Kyle I had seen how he watched out for Jed.

"You know, there's my mom, but she has her own problems, and I really can't talk to her too much. I had my girlfriend, but, well, you know what happened with her. I guess I didn't really love her like I thought. We were just together for so long, I was used to her. And then there was Hunter, but how close can you get to a guy like that?" He laughed sarcastically.

"Yeah, right," I agreed.

"But when Jed moved in, and Rosa asked me to help out, and she told me all that he had been through, it was like I felt like somebody needed me. You know, his life was even more messed up than mine, and

169

I thought…I thought I could be there for him, you know, like someone he looked up to, like a big brother." He turned away, his gaze returning to the ground. "Of course, now I've screwed up so badly that he hates me and he won't even talk to me."

"He'll get over it," I said, trying to sound reassuring.

"I don't know," Kyle answered, shaking his head doubtfully. "Definitely not before I leave. But maybe you could at least talk to him for me. You're the only person he really trusts. Maybe you could tell him that I know I totally screwed up and that I know I'm an asshole. And tell him that I do care about him a lot, and that I'm truly sorry about everything."

I smiled at him and nodded. "Sure," I said. "I can talk to him for you."

"Thanks," he said. "You're a good person, Rachel, a really good person. I could never be as forgiving as you are."

I considered what Kyle had just said to me. Was I really that forgiving? *Maybe*, I thought. Perhaps he was right. But only time would tell if I could ever totally forgive him for everything that had happened.

Chapter 16

That night as I lay in bed, my thoughts turned to what I would say to Jed about Kyle. I knew it would be tough. Jed had nothing good to say about Kyle now, and I expected he would be angry that I had even spoken to him, let alone met with him.

In the morning, I called Jed even earlier than I usually did. "Grab some breakfast and meet me on the pier," I said, feeling somewhat anxious.

"Okay," said Jed. "But how come?"

"Nothing," I lied, "I just want to see you and it's a great morning. Besides, that's where I first met you, and I'm leaving tomorrow, so it'll be sort of nostalgic."

"Yeah, okay," said Jed. "Just let me take a shower and I'll see you there soon."

171

"Bye." I hung up the phone. I had not slept well for worrying about how Jed might react to what I planned to say, and I had been up for several hours when I spoke to him. I had already showered, and I was ready to go. I said good-bye to my grandparents and mounted my bike for the short journey to the pier. It was a morning much like the one when I had first met the boys. I steered the bike down the little main street and occasionally waved at the people as they opened up their stores or waited outside Kelly's for a breakfast table.

The morning sky was a deeper blue than usual, and there were no clouds to be seen in any direction. The gulf waters sparkled under the already bright sun, and as I rode toward its glitter, my heart fluttered with nerves.

I dropped my bike at the end of the pier, and walked along the rough wooden planks leading out into the aqua water. I inhaled the fishy sea air as the seawater sloshed and slapped around the columns beneath me. A seagull cried from the sky above, as a tall, skinny-legged stork that had been standing nearby took slow and deliberate steps away from me.

At the end of the pier, an old man cast his fishing line. His skin was the color of hazelnuts and had the texture of leather. I imagined he had spent his entire life under the Florida sun. Behind him on the bench sat an old woman sipping coffee. The ancient couple did not speak to one another, but I sensed a bond between them, and I wondered how many years they had spent together.

I leaned over the railing and absorbed the view before me. The sunlight danced on the ripples in the water like a thousand fireflies. I did not want to leave this place. I sighed as I acknowledged that I had no choice in the matter. Tomorrow at this time I would be sitting at the airport, waiting to board my plane.

"Hey!" I heard Jed's voice calling to me from the end of the pier. I turned to see him approaching, his old skateboard tucked under his arm. "What's up?" He grinned, waving with his free hand. I smiled and leaned backward, resting my elbows against the railing behind me.

"Hey, baby," he said as he came closer to me. He reached for my face with his caramel-colored hand and gently stroked my skin. "Are you doing okay?" he asked tenderly and with genuine concern.

"Yeah, I'm fine." I smiled, as I put my arm around his waist and pulled his body close to me. He dropped the skateboard and took my face in his hands, lifting it upward to meet his kiss. His lips were soft and gentle, and I closed my eyes so that no other sense would distract me from his warm touch.

"You can't leave me tomorrow," he whispered, still holding my face in his hands.

"I don't want to," I said, as I gazed into the black pools of his almond-shaped eyes.

"Rachel," he said. His voice was full of sadness. "When you go, I'll have no one. I don't know what I'll do without seeing you every day."

"It's going to be the same for me," I said. "But we can e-mail every day. And who knows, maybe I'll be back next year."

"Yeah, I guess," sighed Jed. "But it won't be the same. You don't know how much I'm going to miss you.

"Yes, I do, because I'll miss you, too." I smiled. With his arms around me, I turned and leaned forward against the rail, so that his body was leaning against my back. "Do you remember the day we first met out here on this pier?" I asked him.

"Of course I do," answered Jed. "How could I forget how you started speaking with your English accent, saying things were 'brilliant' and stuff?"

"Yes, exactly, when you made fun of me," I interrupted.

"I did not," objected Jed.

"Yes, you did," I argued. "Then you had a fight with Kyle and went off sulking and we had to go and find you." The instant I mentioned Kyle's name, I felt Jed's body tense.

"Well, Kyle's an asshole, and he's full of crap. He can go to hell for all I care. I wish he'd just left us alone this summer." The tone of his voice was hateful and cold.

I turned around to face him. His expression was one of controlled rage, and I felt some apprehension about pushing the conversation further. But I recalled the pleading in Kyle's voice and the love he had expressed for Jed, and I knew I had to find the courage. "Jed, you know that Kyle loves you," I said. "I know he's made mistakes, but he really cares about you."

"Bullshit," said Jed gruffly, the volume of his voice increasing. "That phony bastard doesn't care about anybody but himself."

"That's not true," I interrupted in Kyle's defense. "He told me himself to tell you how sorry he was and that he knew he had messed up and how much he cares about you." The words spilled out of me and seemed to hit Jed like a freight train. He stepped backward, moving away from me, a look of bewilderment and confusion on his face.

He held his hands out in front of him and cocked his head to the side. "Wait! What did you say? You mean you actually talked to him? When?"

"Last night," I confessed. "But just let me explain."

"What? That bastard called you after what happened?" His voice now expressed obvious fury, and the elderly couple looked at us curiously. He slammed his fist down on the rail of the pier.

"He came over to my house," I said apprehensively. My heart was pounding in my chest, and my mouth was suddenly as dry as a desert. I had known Jed would be upset, but I had not anticipated this degree of reaction, and I felt a little afraid.

"Jesus, Rachel!" Jed's usually tanned face was now red with rage and confusion. "What the hell were you doing with him? What, did you freaking screw him?" He spat the words without looking at me, and his hands gripped the rail so tightly that his knuckles turned white. The old couple who had been watching us gathered their belongings and quickly headed from the pier.

174

"No, it was nothing like that," I cried. I was humiliated and furious that he would accuse me of such a thing. "He just said he needed to talk to me. He wanted to apologize."

"Screw him!" shouted Jed. "He's a liar and he's a frigging asshole who stabbed me in the back when I trusted him. I can't believe you agreed to even see him. What the hell, Rachel? He stood and watched while that freaking pig assaulted you. Why the hell would you listen to a word he says?"

I tried to walk toward him, but he raised his hands in disgust and backed away from me. "That's true," I said. "Everything you said is true. But Kyle's sorry, and he cares about you, you know he does. He loves you, and that's also the truth."

Jed shook his head and started to walk away from me.

"If you walk away from me now, you may never see me again," I called after him in desperation.

He stopped in his tracks and slowly turned to face me. "What do you want from me?" he said, sadly shrugging his shoulders.

"I want you to just listen." I said as I walked toward him. "Just listen to what I have to say." I took his hands in mine and held them as I looked into his sad, dark eyes. He peered back at me, his face perplexed and unsure. His gaze seemed to penetrate me, and I felt my hands squeezing his tighter. Finally he sighed and nodded. "Okay," he said, sounding resigned. "But only because it's you, and I want to trust you. Tell me. Tell me whatever it is you need to say."

We stood on the pier, holding each other's hands while I explained everything that Kyle and I had discussed the night before. Jed listened without interrupting me.

"Are you finished?" he asked after I had stopped speaking. I nodded. "Okay," he said. He let go of my hands and walked a few steps to the rail of the pier. He leaned over, resting his elbows on the wood. I was desperate to hear how he was going to respond to everything I had told him, but I knew it was better for me to hold my tongue at that moment, to give him time to think.

Slowly he turned around and looked at me. He nodded his head. "Okay," he said again. "I believe that nothing happened this time between you two. But that doesn't change anything about how I feel about him. I can't forgive him for what he did with you before, or for what he didn't do to help you."

"What happened between him and me was my fault, too," I argued. "It wasn't like he forced me."

"Yeah, I know that," Jed agreed, the sarcasm apparent in his tone. "But you're only fourteen. Kyle's almost eighteen. He took advantage of you. And what about what happened with that asshole Hunter? What's his excuse for how he acted then?"

"He didn't try to make an excuse," I said somewhat sulkily. I was starting to feel frustrated and hopeless. It seemed that Jed would not be willing to give Kyle another chance, and it saddened me, for I believed in my heart that that would be a mistake. "He didn't make any excuses," I repeated. "But I know that he regrets not doing more now. I think he's learned his lesson. I really do. I really think that the next time he has to stand up to defend someone or something, he will."

Jed shook his head. "You're naive and gullible. He's a selfish bastard and a loser, and I doubt he'll amount to anything."

"You know what I think," I said, the frustration apparent in my tone. "I think you want to hate him because you're scared."

"What are you talking about?" Jed said. I could see he was both annoyed and puzzled by this remark.

"Yes, I think you're scared because tonight he leaves for basic training, and after that you know there's a good chance he'll be deployed to Iraq, or somewhere like that. I think it's easier for you to hate him, and that way, if something bad happens to him, like it did to your mom, it won't hurt so much. If you admit that you love him, and that you need him, then you'll have to worry about him. That's it, isn't it? That's your problem with Kyle."

Jed stared at me, and I could see the pain in his eyes. I knew my words had hurt him deeply, but I believed what I had said to him.

"Tennessee," I said more gently as I walked toward him. "You can't go through life protecting yourself from pain by preventing yourself from feeling love." His sad, young face was pitiful, and he seemed unable to find the words to express his thoughts. He just looked at me and shook his head slowly. "Listen. He's leaving tonight. People are meeting at his house to say good-bye before he catches the bus to North Carolina. I think you should be there."

"No," he said. "You go if you want, but I can't see him. I won't go."

—

For the remainder of the day, Jed and I did not mention Kyle again. Mostly we just held each other. We talked about how we would stay in touch through e-mail and how I hoped I would return next summer. He promised to wait for me, and I promised him the same.

However, as it drew closer to five in the afternoon, I began to feel myself growing increasingly tense. Five was when people were supposed to meet at Kyle's house. He would be leaving for the bus at seven thirty. "Please come, Jed," I begged. "For one thing, I don't want to leave you right now. Plus, I really believe you'll regret it if you don't say good-bye to him."

"I told you," said Jed, as he released me from his embrace and folded his arms across his chest. "I'm not going, I don't want or need to see him, and I won't regret anything."

"Fine," I said in a defeated tone. "But I'm going. I just think it's the right thing to do. I won't stay very long—I just want to say good-

177

bye. I'll come back right after he leaves, and we'll spend the rest of the evening together, okay?"

"Whatever," he responded with a shrug of his shoulders.

I got up from his bed where I had been sitting next to him, and walked toward the door. Before I left the room, I turned to face him. "Jed, I just want you to think about one thing. Just imagine how you would have felt if you had not said good-bye to your mother and you hadn't told her how you felt about her before she left, knowing how she came back."

Jed had been looking down at the floor, but he looked up at me at that moment, and his big, dark eyes revealed his pain. He gazed at me silently, his breathing deep and heavy, and then he opened his mouth as if he was about to says something. But he said nothing, and quickly he turned away, barely shaking his head as he closed his eyes. "Just go," he whispered.

I walked slowly toward Kyle's house, hoping with all my heart that at any moment I would hear Jed's footsteps because he had, in the end, chosen to come with me. I just knew it was the right thing for him to do. But I also understood his anger and frustration with Kyle and how he believed that Kyle had betrayed him. All the misjudgments and the reckless behavior had taken their toll. The damage had been done. And yet deep down, beneath all the pain and disappointment, I believed Jed and Kyle loved and needed each other. I wondered what more I could have done. I had tried to explain. I had tried to heal the wounds. I had begged and I had pleaded. Now it was up to Jed. As I approached Kyle's front door, I looked back one last time, willing Jed to appear. The trees rustled in the darkness and I held my breath, but nobody appeared, and I realized with deep disappointment it had just been the wind.

The mood at Kyle's house was odd. People chatted and laughed, and at first glance it might have appeared that everyone was quite jovial. But there was a heaviness that hung in the air, and I sensed the general feeling in the room to be more somber than celebratory. The setup was that of a party, with chips and drinks and even a cake that said "Good luck," but everybody seemed much more subdued than normal. The usual crowd was present, plus a few faces I did not recognize. Hunter was conspicuously absent, but it didn't appear to me that he was missed.

As I wandered over to help myself to some soda, I overheard Rosa talking with Kyle's mom.

"So, are you ready for this?" Rosa asked Kyle's mother.

She raised her eyebrows and smiled, but her eyes were full of sadness. "Well," she sighed, "he's been with me for almost eighteen years, but I always knew there'd come a time when he would leave me. So I guess I'm ready."

"But he's joining the army at a time of war, Carla," said Rosa.

"Look, Rosa," said Kyle's mom sternly. "You and I have been friends for a long time. I know that you don't agree with what Kyle's doing, but it's his decision, not mine and not yours. It's what he wants, and I can only hope he's doing the right thing. All I can do now is pray that God watches over him. What he and I both need from you is your support, not your criticism."

"He's not even eighteen until next month. You didn't have to give your permission. He could have waited," Rosa scolded.

"Let's not go there," said Carla, shaking her head. "He's my son, my only son. Don't you think I know what's at risk? But I did what I believed was right at the time, and I have to live with that decision, so let's just leave it at that."

Okay, you're right," conceded Rosa. "It's not my business. I really wasn't meaning to criticize you. It's just that I care about Kyle as if he were my own, and remember, I know how it feels to lose an only child. Tennessee's father was about Kyle's age when he was killed, you know."

"I know that. And I can't imagine how it must have felt. I just try not to think about it."

179

"I know, honey. And I don't like to think about it either. But I'm older than you, and I remember the Vietnam War." There was a long pause, as if both women were contemplating the implications of the conversation. I, too, was imagining what might be waiting for Kyle in the future, and the possibilities scared and saddened me.

"Look, I'm sorry, Carla," said Rosa abruptly, finally breaking the heavy silence between them. "I shouldn't be talking to you like this now. It's not fair of me. Please forgive me. I know if anyone will be okay, it'll be Kyle."

Carla nodded but looked unconvinced. "Don't worry about it," she said. She turned away from Rosa and her eyes met mine.

"Hi, chick, how are you doing?"

"I'm okay," I answered.

"And where's my grandson?" asked Rosa. "He's usually stuck to your hip. Have you two had a falling-out or something?"

"No," I replied. I tried to come up with an excuse for Jed's absence, but my mind seemed to stall, and I couldn't think of a single good reason. Fortunately at that moment Kyle approached and the subject was quickly forgotten. "Hi, Rachel," said Kyle. "Thanks for coming by."

"Sure," I said. I looked at him, observing his handsome young face. We had been through so much together over these last few months. I wondered if I'd ever see him again after today.

"Come here, kid," said Rosa, smiling widely. "Give your Aunt Rosa one of those big bear hugs you do so well." Rosa opened her arms to receive Kyle in an embrace. He smiled at her, and the two of them hugged. It was obvious to anyone watching that they had grown to care for each other deeply over the years. "Now you listen to your Aunt Rosa, *mi hijo*," she said, as she released him. "You were a great kid, and you've grown into a fine young man. Now, I'm not going to lie about how I feel about you signing up, because you know all too well that I don't like the idea. But I know that you've got a good heart." Rosa reached out and touched Kyle's chest. "And I know that no matter what, you'll always do the right thing and stand up for what's right." Kyle glimpsed at me from the corner of his eyes. "Look at me, Kyle," commanded Rosa. "You make sure you take care of yourself off at boot camp or whatever you call it these days, and if, God forbid, you're sent out into combat, you make sure you wear that body armor and you keep that pretty head low. Do we understand each other?"

Kyle looked into Rosa's eyes. Her face was deadly serious. "Yes, ma'am," he said with conviction. He then turned to his mother, who wiped the tears from her green eyes that were identical to her son's. "It's okay, Mom," he said gently, as he took her in his arms. She laid her head on his shoulder and wept, and the sound of her sobbing filled the quiet room.

The time passed quickly. I frequently looked toward the front door hoping to see Jed, but he didn't come. It was almost time for Kyle to leave. He walked over to me and led me away from Brook and Tyler with whom I had been chatting. "Excuse me, guys," he apologized to them. "I need to talk to Rachel a second."

We stepped out the front door into the hot and humid night air. "Did you get to talk to Jed?"

"Yeah, I did. I told him everything you told me to."

He sighed heavily. "I guess he's still not coming, then. He still really hates me, doesn't he?"

"I don't know," I said, shaking my head. I felt so sorry for him. He looked so lost and helpless at that moment. "It's been a lot for him to handle, you know. You have to understand how upset he was about you joining the army in the first place."

He sighed and nodded. "Yeah, I know."

"Kyle, baby," Carla called.

"I'll be right there, Mom," he yelled in reply. The front door opened and Carla appeared.

"Baby, we've got to go if you're going to make that bus," she said.

"Yeah, okay," sighed Kyle. "I'm ready." Kyle followed his mother back into the house. He turned to look back at me before closing the door. "Are you coming?" he asked.

"No, I'll just stay here for now." I leaned backward against the house wall and drew the wet night air slowly into my lungs. Kyle would be gone in a few minutes. I could feel a lump swelling in my throat. I wasn't ready. I wasn't ready to say good-bye to him. I wasn't ready to say good-bye to Jed. Everything seemed unfinished, like it was all ending too soon, and yet I was powerless to stop it.

The front door opened, and Kyle stepped out into the night. On his shoulder, he carried a duffel bag that appeared to be almost busting at the seams. He walked toward the driveway and was followed by the crowd from inside the house. The well-wishers gathered around him, and the farewells began. "Take it easy, man. Stay cool, brother," said Tyler as he hugged Kyle powerfully and slapped him on his back.

"Yeah, sure, and you take care of little Brook here." Kyle winked at Brook as she wiped a tear from her cheek.

"Come here, you big jerk," she sniffed, as she wrapped her arms around his waist and laid her head on his chest. "We'll miss you."

The hugging, high-fiving, and fist-bumping continued, as I waited apprehensively for my chance to say good-bye. When Kyle approached me, I had to swallow hard to stop myself from crying. He stood before me and smiled, opening his arms for a hug. His body was warm and sweaty, and I was suddenly overwhelmed by the tremendous tenderness I felt toward him. He leaned down to whisper in my ear. "Jed's a lucky guy" was all he said.

After hugging me, Kyle moved on to Rosa. She looked up into his face and smiled. "Remember what I told you." He drew her close to him and squeezed, lifting her feet from the ground. "Put me down right now," she said, giggling. He lowered her down and kissed her on the cheek. "Bye," he whispered.

Kyle's mother had been watching the whole time, smiling and patiently waiting to drive her only son to the bus station. "Are you ready now, kiddo?" she asked.

"Yeah, let's go," replied Kyle assertively. "I'll drive." He walked to the back of the car and opened the trunk, throwing his bag in carelessly.

"Kyle." The voice in the darkness behind him seemed to startle him. He turned abruptly.

"Jed," he said, as Jed stepped into the light of the streetlamp.

Jed looked up into Kyle's face. "Hey, man."

"I'm glad you decided to show," said Kyle.

"You're such a dick," said Jed, his eyes narrowed.

"Yeah, I know," Kyle said, nodding. The two boys eyed each other without saying another word for several seconds.

"Look, Jed, I'm sorry," began Kyle.

Jed's lips began to tremble and his eyes filled with tears. "I don't want you to go," he said in a cracked voice. "Just don't go."

Now Kyle's eyes began to well with tears. "Shit, now you're making me cry in front of my boys, kid." His lips trembled as he smiled. "You're going to be fine without me, little brother," he said. "You're a stronger man than I'll ever be. I have no doubt that you'll succeed in everything you do. You know I love you, right?"

The two boys wrapped their arms around each other and hugged for a moment. Then Kyle released Jed and pushed him away. "Now go on back to your girl." He nodded his head in my direction. "She's waiting for you." He turned to his mother. "Come on, Mom."

Kyle and his mother got into the car. As he pulled the car out of the driveway, he leaned out the open window. His green eyes sparkled and he grinned widely, showing all his white teeth. "Bye, losers," he yelled, and then the car sped away.

As it disappeared around the bend, Rosa approached her grandson. She put her arm around him and asked if he was all right.

"I will be," answered Jed.

183

I walked over to him and smiled. "Well," I said. "I guess that's it. He's gone. I think you did the right thing by coming to say good-bye.

"Yeah," agreed Jed. "Do you want to get out of here?" I nodded.

"We're going back over to our house, Rosa," said Jed to his grandmother.

"Sure, Tennessee," she answered. "Go and relax in the time you have left together. I have to stick around and lock up for Carla, all right?"

Jed and I strolled back to his house, where we opted to sit outside in Rosa's beautiful little garden. We sat together on the little garden swing and held hands as we rocked back and forth. "You were right," said Jed. "About Kyle, I mean."

"Well, it was obvious how much you care about each other," I said.

"I wish he hadn't joined the army." He looked at me, his eyes wide and full of honesty. "I really don't think he knows what he's getting into."

"I think you're wrong, Jed," I said. "I think he knows exactly what he's doing and what he could lose." We sat together without speaking for a long while. The only sound was the sound of the crickets and the squeak of the rocking swing. Jed let go of my hand and put his arm around me, gently caressing my shoulder with his fingers.

"Jed," I said. "Remember how I said you shouldn't be afraid to love someone just because something might happen to them or you might not see them again?"

"Yeah, and you were right, I told you before," interrupted Jed.

"Yes, but I was thinking. Maybe it's the same with me. Maybe I was afraid to, you know, be with you because I have to leave and I might not see you again. Maybe…" I hesitated. "Maybe we should, before I leave. I'm not afraid anymore."

Jed turned to look at me. He lowered his lips to mine and kissed me tenderly. "No," he said. "I know you're not afraid, and you shouldn't be. And there is nothing I would like more than to be with you, Rachel. But not like that, not now."

"What do you mean, not like that?" I asked.

"What I mean is that you don't have to do something you're not sure about just to prove that you care about me."

"But maybe I am sure. Maybe it's what I want. I feel ready now."

He smiled. "Well, maybe you are ready, and maybe it's me who's not. Now I'm the one who's not sure." He paused for a second as if he was considering my proposition. He sighed and shook his head. "I just think we should leave things the way they are. The way they are right now, right here, with you and me together on this swing, in this garden, I feel like everything is perfect. Do you get what I mean?"

I nodded without speaking. I knew what he was saying because at that moment I was sure that I was feeling exactly what he was feeling.

"I just don't want anything to mess up tonight."

I smiled at him and sighed. "So you're sure?"

"Yeah, I might regret it tomorrow, but I'm sure." He sighed and pulled me close as he rocked the swing back and forth with his feet. "God knows, I really love you, and I hope more than anything we'll be together again someday. I can wait for you until then. Can you wait for me?"

I took a long, deep breath, enjoying the sweet, pungent aromas of all the flowers from Rosa's garden. "Well, actually…" I turned my face to look at him. "I really love you, too. I mean it. And I know that we will be together again one day, because I'll make sure of it. And so, to answer your question, yes, I'll wait for you. I promise."

I could see the love and contentment in Jed's face as he began to speak. "You are an amazing person, Rachel, and you have so much more strength than you realize. I don't know if you see it in yourself, but I do." He tapped my left chest with the tips of his fingers. "Here in your heart, you have the courage to let yourself feel, to dream, and believe. You're not afraid to speak up when you have to, and you're willing to forgive, which is something that most people have a really hard time with. You saved my life, I know you did. You probably saved Kyle, too, in a way."

"Thank you, Tennessee," I said, not really sure how I should respond to his compliment. He spoke with such intense certainty, that I did not doubt for one second that he believed his own words. But did I believe them? I had always felt there was something about Jed that was wise beyond his years, and I had to consider the possibility that he might be right. Maybe, just maybe I *was* strong and courageous and all the other things he had said about me. I smiled at the thought as I breathed in the warm night air. *He's right about one thing for sure*, I thought. *Tonight everything is perfect, and tomorrow will be a brand-new day.* What tomorrow would bring I didn't know. But I was sure of one thing—Tennessee loved me, and no matter what happened, my Tennessee Jed would be waiting for me.